MW01049529

Forever Land –
the Four Wonders
By Brooklyn Ver Beek

To:
Heather Hart Dickerson
For being a great language arts teacher,
Jennifer Cousins for helping me put myself
out there
and Dustin Ver Beek for helping Forever
Land come to life·

Forever Land – The Four Wonders

Contents

Forever Land the Four Wonders

Introduction
(England 1985)

Isaac lay in his bed, staring out the tiny screen window across the room. He could make out a couple of stars in the distance. They were so hard to see, even though his bed was closest.

"Levi! Stop kicking your mattress you dive me crazy listening to you!" Max whispered furiously as he threw himself back in bed.

"Well it's not my fault, I'm bored!" Levi responded bitterly.

"Will you two be quiet? You are going to wake professor Macmillan up and get us in trouble!" Samantha said crossly in a hushed voice.

Max glared at Levi and tossed his small throw pillow at the end of the bed. Levi rolled his eyes and crawled under the sheets and hid down there. Isaac rolled over on his side. It was so difficult, being an orphan. You were always herded around like sheep. Isaac had constantly wondered why it was them who ended up at Iron Gates Orphanage. But he knew why, for a fact. His parents had left.

They had left him, Max, Levi and Samantha at this dump.

Well most people didn't know Isaac was related to them. He had dark brown hair that slicked down his forehead as bangs. He had brown eyes that were always wide open whenever he was awake. And he wore glasses. Whereas Levi had light blonde hair that had spiky bangs in the front, blue eyes and a very wide smile. And as for Max and Samantha, they were twins. Both had dirty blonde hair, both were fairly tall, but Samantha had green eyes and Max, blue. The twins were twelve, Levi, thirteen, and Isaac was fourteen, well, not for long. His birthday was tomorrow and then he'd be fifteen. Every year on his birthday, he would wish that he and his siblings could find a way out of Iron Gates Orphanage. And this year, he knew that he would make the same wish. Little did he know his wish would come true.

Forever Land – The Four Wonders

Chapter 1

The Three Gifts

Ding- Dong! The bell rang. " Ugh!" Isaac groaned, getting out of bed and pushing his glasses on. He looked around the dim room. There were no moving bumps inside the other beds. They were already made and fresh looking. That's strange, Isaac thought as he looked around the room once more. Then, he grinned. Two packages laid at the foot of his bed. One package was small and lumpy, and the other was big and felt rather strange.

Red ribbons were tied around each of them. The package paper was really just scraps of taped together newspaper. A note was tied to each. Isaac reached for the smaller package first, untied the note from the ribbon, and read it.

Dear Isaac, I hope you enjoy this present dearly because it will come

in handy in around a month.

Your loving sister, Samantha.

Isaac pulled the ribbon from the package, tore the newspaper off and grinned. It was a long, red scarf. Perfect, he thought. He laid the scarf gently on the bed and opened the letter to the next package.

Dear Isaac,
I know your going to love this present just as much as the
we gave you last year. Love, Max and Levi.

Isaac snorted with laughter. Last year, Max and Levi had given him an old macaroni necklace and a rusty nail clipper. He opened the present and gasped. Inside was a new jackknife and a fancy pouch for it. The reason why the package felt so hard, was because the newspaper had been wrapped around a stiff shoe box.

I wonder where they this all. Isaac thought. Then, he noticed a small paragraph at the bottom of the letter.

PS, we over slept and rushed down to Science class without waking you up, sorry!

Isaac jumped out of bed and raced for the closet to

pull on his orphanage school robes. He stuck on the badge that said 'United We Stand' in gold letters. They didn't wake him up?! How could they?! Professor Macmillan would be furious! She never forgave those who were tardy. Isaac dashed out the door and raced down the hallway as he clutched his books tightly to his chest.

Several older children looked at him oddly as he ran down the hall narrowly avoiding every creepy portrait and knight statue. Soon enough he was met with the classroom door. He knew how Professor Macmillan would react when he appeared.

Slowly and nervously, he opened the door. It creaked so loudly that almost the whole class looked up at him. Some even dropped their pencils bouncing off their wooden desks.

Standing in the far east corner, was Professor Macmillan. She slowly lay down her book, removed her small spectacles, and rushed past every desk until she was staring into Isaac's eyes. She was almost his height, she had short, curly white blonde hair with two green bows on both sides near her ears. Her eyes were dark blue, and her features were pointed.

"You're late" she said in a deadly mutter. Her eyes dancing with fury, "Where were you?!" she demanded.

"I...I..." but Professor Macmillan smiled nastily and finished for him. " You were just- *magically* late were you."

Isaac glared at Levi, Max and Samantha who sat near the front row, looking nervously at him.

"Get to your seat!" Professor Macmillan ordered, pointing to the seat next to Levi.

Isaac slowly walked over to where Professor Macmillan was pointing and sat down, not looking at any of his siblings. Professor Macmillan slammed her ruler on the board revealing a picture of the solar system, she cleared her throat and the lesson began.

As they opened their text books, Levi leaned over and whispered, "Happy Birthday..."

Chapter 2

Professor Amy

"Why didn't you wake me up?!" Isaac mumbled near the end of the day, now figuring that it was pointless trying to ignore his siblings all day long.

"We thought you'd wake up only a little moment after us, but we tried waking you up, and we thought you heard us, so we went." Samantha explained calmly.

"Well, I guess the presents stalled you then?" Max asked.

Isaac rolled his eyes and said sarcastically. "Yeah, something like that."

"Well, did you like the presents at least?" Levi asked hopefully.

Isaac sighed and smiled a bit. "Yeah, thanks."

Samantha tried to change the subject. "Well, we

have a test in arithmetic Thursday, we should probably study."

All three boys groaned, "Samantha, we've been writing all day! Show us some mercy!"

"Besides..." Max said, "I have got to finish the art project Professor Amy assigned."

Samantha gasped, "Max, that's due tomorrow!" she said very panicky.

Max rolled his eyes. "Don't you think I know that?!" he retorted.

Just then, Professor Amy exited the school office and was walking toward them. "Oh, Professor Amy!!!" Samantha called.

Amy smiled and walked over to them. "Evening, Isaac, Levi, Max, and Samantha." she sweetly greeted them,"How are you all?"

"Well, most of us are okay..." Levi shot a grin at Max, who blushed.

"How are you, Professor?" Samantha asked politely in return.

"Quite well, it's just that I was walking down the hall, when I noticed a peculiar dark cloud." she explained. The boys grinned awkwardly.

Samantha tried to break the silence. "Er... Professor Amy, do you have my book repaired? I mean... not trying to come off rude, it's just that I'm at this fascinating part." Amy laughed and pulled from her burlap bag, a small black book that imprinted the words, ' Tale of the Lost Boy.' and handed it to her.

"Thank you!" she smiled.

Amy nodded and gasped at Isaac. "Oh I almost forgot! Isaac, you're turning fifteen!"

Isaac blushed a bit. "Yeah..." he slowly said.

Amy smiled and pulled out a beautiful throw pillow and handed it to Isaac. "I made it a couple days ago. Luckily remembered to give it to you. Happy Birthday."

Isaac stared at the pillow. Painted on the front, was a picture of his parents, both smiling. "Th-- Thanks." he stuttered.

Amy smiled. "Your parents were my best friends, they were such good people."

Isaac tried not to frown. "Then... why did they leave us?" he asked.

Amy suddenly had a sad look on her face. "Isaac... they..." she looked down and drew a quivery breath.

Samantha looked at Amy and then to the boys who had blank expressions on their faces. "It's a lovely gift Professor."

Amy smiled rather meekly. "Good. I added a touch of ma- I mean I added some sprinkle glue... er... to make the tassels look a little more lively."

The four looked awkwardly at each other and waited for someone to say something else. "It is outstanding, Professor..." Samantha said kindly.

"No wonder you're our art teacher!" Levi said.

Amy broke into gales of laughter. But just then thunder crashed and Amy looked strangely out the window. "Looks like it's going to rain." she quietly said.

Samantha looked around, seeming to find something to say. "Well, we don't want to be rude or anything, but we best be going."

Amy stood there for a moment then smiled. "Oh, alright then... goodbye." she said as she then began walking away.

"Thanks again!" Isaac called after her. But there was no response. Levi checked around the corner and saw that it was completely empty.

"Strange..." said Isaac.

"Who cares! Let's go eat, I'm starving!" Levi groaned as his stomach growled.

"As usual..." Samantha chuckled, and they walked down the hallway and finally, they made it into the dining hall. Most people were already seated and waiting patiently while the teachers were talking in whispers on the north side of the great room.

Once they sat down next to a few teenage girls, who made faces and quickly scooted away. The four weren't very popular. Professor Macmillan started walking up the stairs once she shouted "let the feast begin!" Kids scrambled for the plates of food and started stuffing their faces. Isaac held a large turkey leg and went munching away. Levi griped a roll as butter slid out before he bit into it. Max held his spoon like a dagger and stuffed a large mouthful of mashed potatoes in.

"So what did you get for your birthday?" Isaac's friend Riley asked curiously. Riley was Isaac's only friend. Isaac nodded and pulled the pillow out from his robes. Riley's eyes went wide and he grinned showing his brown teeth.

"I'm assuming Professor Amy gave that to you." he assumed brightly.

Isaac, his mouth finally empty, answered, "It's so obvious though nobody could do art that well." Everyone at the table laughed. Even Samantha.

Just then, the doors at the top of the stairs swung open and down came Professor Macmillan and Professor Amy. "I think you're crazy, Amy!" Professor Macmillan hissed, "There is nobody named Dietomorse coming to abuse our orphanage!" They could hear Professor Amy trying to reason with her, but she seemed to be failing. Everyone was deathly quiet, but once the shouting stopped, everyone went back to their food. No one wanted to get in trouble. But the four and Riley all looked at one another, not saying a word.

"She's really angry...Professor Amy." Riley said quietly, taking a small bite of fluffy potato.

Samantha looked at the boys who were staring down the hall in a daze. "Let's go to bed." Samantha suggested. The boys nodded and stood up to leave the crowded dine hall with their sister.

At last, all the halls were quiet and still.

Chapter 3

The Secret Home

"It was funny to hear a booming noise when it wasn't even raining." Max said that night.

"It's raining right now genius!" Levi retorted.

"Yes, but it wasn't earlier." Samantha said as she read her book,
"Hey, could I talk to you guys for a moment?"

"You always do..." Isaac murmured, half smiling.

Samantha sat up in bed, "Don't you think that professor Amy was acting a little weird earlier?"

Max chuckled. "She's been acting weird ever since we could understand English." he joked.

Levi looked a him. "We could always speak English, what do you think we are, Korean?" then he laughed.

Samantha shook her head. "I wonder what was going on with her and Professor Macmillan..." "It had something to do with this man named Dieto...Ditto...Oh, I can't remember." Levi sighed.

Samantha looked down, "Well, whoever he is, he sounds pretty dangerous."

Isaac got out of bed, "She's right." he said as he sat by the window sill. "What are you doing?" Levi asked. Isaac stroked his pillow, "Looking..." he mumbled, "At the stars."

Levi shrugged and then got up too. "I wonder if this Dietom... whatever his name is... was a murderer..."

Samantha sighed, "He could be... It's just that- Isaac, are you alright?"

The three turned to Isaac, who was backing away from the window slowly with a terrified look on his face.

"What's the ma-" Samantha's voice died away when she looked out the window and she too, started backing away, slowly falling downward. Max and Levi were looking at one another until Levi had looked out the window and his mouth dropped open. Max was almost hiding under the blankets, but Levi grabbed his arm and pulled him down next to the others who were all pressed into the corner of the room.

They all stared horrifyingly out the window. Replacing the rainy sky, was a dark gray cloud that nearly covered the entire sky. There was no rain, but there was lightning and thunder coming from some clouds. And, upon the darkest cloud, was man in a black cloak that hid his entire face. He was yelling words that the four couldn't understand. He held a silver wand that shot red lightning out from it. He was getting closer and closer. When he was almost upon them, Amy burst through the doors and pulled from her sleeve, a spruce wood wand and pointed it at the evil man.

"Recomarado!!!" she cried and the man and dark sky all but disappeared in a flash.

Amy stood there taking shallow breaths, still pointing at the window. Then, once she realized what she was doing, she quickly slipped her wand back down her sleeve and turned to the four, who pressed as far as they could against the wall. If they could've went inside the wall they would have. "No..." she whispered, "Don't be afraid."

Isaac stood up right away shaking, "Then what was *that* all about?!"

Amy squinted and approached closer, "I just happened to save your life young man!" she said firmly.

The other three stood up. "Who was that?!" Max asked, still staring out the window.

Amy sat down on one of the beds.

"That was Dietomorse, he's a dark spirit, well... no one really...He"

Samantha interrupted her, "So you're a-"
"Wizard..."

Amy finished, "Yes."

"What was he doing?" Max asked.

Amy didn't answer, instead she stood up and looked anxiously at them. "Listen, Dietomorse is after you! Ever since the night he-he-" tears rolled down her cheeks as she looked at them all, "Since the night he killed your parents."

Shocked looks appeared on the fours faces.

"Really?" Isaac asked. Amy nodded,

"So now he came here to try and kill you and I have no choice but to send you away... you'll have to go..."

"Go?" Levi demanded, "Go where?"

Amy sniffed, "To Forever Land."

Chapter 4

The F.L Express

"Professor Amy, for the fifth time, what is Forever Land?" Samantha impatiently asked as she, Amy and the boys ran down the quiet street. Few street lamps were lit, so they had to carry lanterns.

"Not now, Samantha, I need to get you and the boys to Mel." They were nearing the city gate exit and Amy began looking for the right key.

"Who's Mel?" Max asked curiously. Amy unlocked the gate and held it open for the four to go through.

"Driver of F.L express." she answered quickly.

Levi looked ahead, "Which means?"

Amy smiled a bit. "Forever Land Express."

Max sighed, "How do we find this Mel and his Forever Land Express?" he asked.

Samantha looked oddly at him, "Like all other expresses, the train station."

And sure enough, through the dark pine trees, they saw a dim light. Perfect, they thought. They went inside the train station which was abandoned and lonely looking. Amy and the four hastily crossed the tracks and sat down on the waiting benches.

"Mel should be here at any moment." said Amy, checking her pocket watch. Looking up, she smiled at the kids, "Don't worry." she reassured them, "You'll be alright."

"But won't Dietomorse find us? Doesn't he *live* in Forever Land?" Samantha asked.

Amy nodded, "Yes, but you'll be protected. Dustin Sparks is there and is just as powerful as Dietomorse." she answered calmly.

"Who's Dustin Sparks?" asked Isaac.

Amy grinned, "You'll like him. He's the king of Forever Land basically, but owns Wizard Land." "There are lands?!" Max exclaimed.

"Yes." Amy chuckled. "There is the Sioux Village, Pirates Cove, Wizard Land, Grandly Forest-" "What's the most dangerous spot in Forever Land in your opinion?"

Amy thought for a moment, "Well... I don't necessarily fancy Black Forest."
Just then, a shrilling scream was heard and there was Dietomorse, who had appeared on the other side of the track and started across toward them, when a sudden roar filled the air. Two lights appeared from inside the dark tunnel, and there was the train.

It had 'Forever Land Express' imprinted in gold letters on the front and looked beautiful on the black and red car. The car screeched to a halt and the doors opened. In the drivers seat was an old man. He had pointy features, gray hair that stuck up all over the place and a stringy gray mustache. Not to mention he looked tall and bony and his clothes were tattered and dirty.

"Howdy there, boy, it sure is great to finally meet you!" the man cheerfully greeted them.

Levi turned to Professor Amy. "How does he know us?"

Amy looked from Mel to Levi. "Mel will explain along the way..." she assured.

"Forever Land, I presume?" Mel asked gazing at Amy.

"Yes..." Amy sighed. "On you go, sweet children."

Samantha hugged her tightly. "Will we ever see you again?" she asked.

Amy started to softly cry. "Of course you will! I promise someday we will see each other again."

Samantha let go of her and boarded the train along with her brothers.

Amy spoke to Mel for quite some time. The four could not hear what they spoke about, but it appeared to be important. Both nodding, Mel finally closed the train doors. Slowly, the train started lunging forward. The four looked out the dirty window of their booth. Dietomorse was gone; for now.

Relieved, they all waved to Amy, who waved back. They kept waving, until they couldn't see a glimpse of her. A heavy sadness filled the train car as the four realized their lives had just changed forever.

Chapter 5

The Train Ride

The train was moving so quickly now that the four didn't really feel like looking out the windows. This train was very abnormal. It didn't run on tracks, and Mel didn't really seem to be watching his driving and the train didn't falter.

"So is there really such thing as this Forever Land?" Max asked.

Mel looked into the mirror, "Well of course there is!" he answered in a raspy voice, "I have been there myself and driving to it now about five hundred thousand times!" he said.

"Oh, what do the people look like?" Samantha asked.

Mel scratched his gray whiskers and turned right, "Well, the wizards wear long cloaks and robes and always wear pointy hats and almost always carry wands. As for the Indians, well, they wear buffalo and deer hides with leather moccasins. And the pirates always wear rags for clothes but have shiny bling and carry around swords as long as a mans arm. And-"

"Well ,what are you then?" Levi interrupted.

Mel chuckled, "Oh, I'm no Forever Land citizen, I'm just the conductor."

"Why are we so important to Forever Land?" Isaac asked, leaning forward.

Mel looked in the mirror and smiled, "Cause yer the special ones...that's why."

The four looked at each other "Us?...Special?...No!" they blurted in agreement.

Mel seemed shocked, "Why sure!" he responded, "Yer parents were great people, yer mum was the first human to enter Forever Land and later on she had you four and then you randomly disappeared that night-" Mel paused. "I said too much..."

The four all looked at each other dumbfounded.

"Anyways... Amy told us about this man called Dustin Sparks and he rules Forever Land, what is he like?" Samantha asked. Mel grinned showing his buck teeth.

"He's a good man that Dustin Sparks. He has a name for you! The Four Wonders!" Mel answered. "He's powerful, kind, wise, and so much more..."

Samantha sighed. "Well I'd sure love to meet him..."

"Yeah..." Max agreed.

Levi nodded and Isaac leaned against the window. He looked down and realized that the train was moving on top of the sea. He looked out and saw a small green mountain peak in the cloudy sky rising out of the deep blue waters. As it came closer and closer, it became clear they were headed to a large island! The island was a most beautiful sight; almost like heaven.

All of a sudden, Mel cried out, "We're here! We made it to Forever Land!"

Chapter 6

Grandly Forest

"Alright children, step on out, careful for snapping grass!!!" Mel ordered as the four eagerly climbed down the steps.

"Snapping grass?" Levi questioned as he got down. Mel nodded and pointed to a plant that seemed to be just coming up from the ground; bright red with teeth and a green stem. It rose only about eight inches from the ground and snapped at a passing fly.

"Whoa..." Isaac murmured in amazement.

"Ye don't wanna go near any o those." Mel warned them, "They're poisonous." Mel raised both arms and announced, "Welcome to Grandly Forest!"

Isaac smiled as Mel handed them a map, "Thank you for all the trouble!" he grinned.

"Anytime!" Mel replied, "Be safe!"

"Bye!" the four called as they entered the Grandly Forest. Mel waved and got back on the train and soon was mysteriously gone.

~

So they started walking, not knowing what else to do. A few hours had passed and the four were still walking, they were tired, hungry, and thirsty.

"All I want right now is a table full of turkey legs, mashed potatoes, fudge squares, and chocolate marshmallow cookies!" Max whined.

"Oh shut up! If anything, I'd love to have hundreds of crystal glasses filled with nutmeg!" Samantha snapped. Isaac looked at the never ending path of trees ahead.

"Good Lord, if I wanted anything, I'd choose a king sized bed with Egyptian cotton sheets and puffy pillows and a warm fireplace!" he moaned.

Levi groaned, "Just stop it! This nonsense about imaginary essentials will just make us even more crazy than what we already are!"

"Hey, smoke!"

"I said stop it Max!"

"No really, smoke!" Max was pointing at huge puff clouds of smoke ahead, surrounded by pine trees.

"Oh, thank heavens!" Samantha cried gratefully, "It could possibly be a house of some sort, maybe whoever lives there, can help us! Come on!" Samantha, Isaac and Max all started toward the smoke when Levi shouted,

'STOP!!!' The three turned to face Levi, neither had smiles on their faces. Levi approached them quietly,

"Are you all mad?! What if it could be... An Indian camp?" Everyone looked at each other, wide eyed.

"He's right..." Isaac mumbled.

Levi huddled everyone together, "Okay, here's what we'll do, we'll go quietly around the camp, and meet wherever we can, and if they see us, we run."

Even though the plan was stupid, they all nodded and crept forward. Isaac felt his throat go tight. But he gasped aloud when he saw that it wasn't an Indian camp! It was just a small white cottage with small red shutters.

Chapter 7

The Dwarf and the Story

"It's not an Indian camp, you idiot!" Isaac called annoyingly, coming out from the trees.

"Well I'm sorry! It's not a bad thing to worry!" Levi responded bitterly. "Let's just see if anyone's in there!" The white cottage looked bent over a bit and sat in the middle of a lush clearing.

"Whoever it is, I hope they'll be able to help us..." Samantha mumbled. The four walked onto the porch and realized how small the door was. It went only up to Levi's waist. They all looked oddly at each other and Max knocked on the door. It made a very hollow noise as it echoed among the woods. No answer. Max tried again, and then came a little voice,

"Coming!" It called.

The four backed away a little as the door slowly opened. And there stood a little old woman, she was wrinkled but had a kind face. The little old woman had short curly brownish hair that sat under a white bonnet and a dutch looking costume. She looked very surprised to see them.

"The Four Wonders! Such an honor!" she exclaimed.

Levi stepped in between them, "For the love of cripe! Why does everyone call us that?!"

The woman chuckled, "Well Dustin Sparks calls you that! Great man he is, so wise, and he wonders about you four, so great as well." she smiled pleasantly. Then a shocked look came on her face. "Oh heavens! I must introduce myself, Lowe Baker, but people call me B's."

Samantha smiled, "Pleased to meet you, B's. I'm Samantha and these are my brothers, Isaac, Levi and Max VerBeek." she kindly responded.

B's smiled then said, "Would you like to come in?"

"Please!" the four all responded almost at once. B's moved out of the way to let them in, the four had to crouch down to get through the door. It was very dark inside, until B's clapped her hands and dozens of candles went on and so did a warm fireplace. The four looked at B's, astounded.

"Please! Have a seat by the table! You must have had a long journey and will continue, you all must be starving!" B's assured them as she waddled over to the kitchen. The four eagerly sat down at the small wooden table and waited for B's to return from her small, little kitchen.

Everything was so tidy and neat and it felt so welcoming. There was a furry chair by the cobblestone fireplace in the living room. And a red and white throw rug beneath it. And the kitchen was accompanied with a small stove, pantry and counter. There was also a wooden staircase that lead to an upstairs.
A few picture frames hung on the walls. There was a picture of a boy and a girl running up a hill together, and another of a wizard wand flashing sparks. One picture really caught their attention. It was a picture of some sort of symbol; vines crossing over each other until it formed some what of a flower.

"Excuse me, B's, what is that picture over there?" Max asked.

B's leaned out the kitchen door to see where Max was pointing. She smiled proudly, "That is the Grandly Forest symbol." she answered. When she saw the fours confused faces, she explained, "Every Forever Land province, has a symbol." she pointed at the map, "Look for yourself." she said excitedly, pointing to the map.

The four leaned over to look at the map and they saw it. On Grandly Forest, there was the same symbol as there was on the picture frame. There were other symbols too. Pirates Cove, had two skulls crossed over on a heavy rope, The Sioux Village had three tepees that were in a formation like a windmill and there were flames sprouting from each one. Wizard Land's symbol almost looked like the British Flag, except circular and several white X's bordering around it. Then, they saw Black Forest symbol, which was a storm cloud that had a bolt of lightning shooting out and a silver sword crossing through it. It formed like an X.

"Dietomorse created that symbol himself." B's said.

Samantha sighed. "Our Professor, Amy, told us that he killed our parents." B's looked surprised,

"Amy?! I haven't heard from that girl in years!"

"You knew her?" Isaac exclaimed. B's nodded,

"Yes." she answered. "Oh! The cakes are ready!" she scurried over to the oven and took out a tray of some really strange cakes. She slid them onto the big plate set out in the middle of the table and let the four take two each. They licked their lips. The cakes were golden brown, with strawberry jelly in the middle and drizzled in icing.

When they each took a bite, their eyes lit up as icing smeared their lips.

"These-r-so-good." Max said with his mouthful. Samantha licked her lips and asked,

"What are these cakes called?" B's looked at her cookbook and answered,

"Jelly Hearts." she answered. She poured tea into four china tea cups and sat down next to the four. "So, where are you from?"

Isaac cleared his throat after swallowing his tea, "We're from England." he answered.

B's seemed interested already. "What is England? Is it in Forever Land?" Levi almost laughed out loud but Samantha kicked his shin from under the table.

"No, no it's far away from here." she responded as she glanced a scolding look at Levi who shrugged.

B's grinned thoughtfully, "Does it get lovely sunshine like we do here?"

Max nodded, "It rains too. But otherwise despite the cold, we do have it good in England."

Samantha nodded in agreement. "Yes and the nights are so starry and beautiful." B's smile broadened.

"I know your mother liked it here too, she had told me a little about what England was like, I just couldn't remember at all."

Isaac's eyes grew wide, "She was here? In Grandly Forest?!"

B's chuckled. "Yes, yes! She loved it here in Grandly Forest!"

Samantha looked down. "What was our mother like to the people here?"

B's slowly looked out the window, "Oh, your mother Lindy was a hero here!" she answered happily. She frowned and sighed a bit. "That night when Dietomorse killed your parents, a great storm came here, in Forever Land. But everyone knew what happened automatically. They also knew that somewhere, Lindy and Jack VerBeek had children. And they would one day see you to return to Forever Land!" she looked back and smiled at the four, who smiled back, "I'm not really the one to be telling you this. That's for Dustin Sparks to explain." she said, waddling to the fire to sit down.

"Just... why are we special?" Levi asked.

B's chuckled again. "We knew that your parents were great and that when you'd return, you'd raise Forever Land up and save us from Dietomorse." she answered gently.

Samantha looked at her brothers who sat with understanding looks on their faces. Then she asked, "Why is Amy in England and not here?"

B's looked surprised again, "How did you-"

"We figured." Max interrupted.

41

B's looked down as she rocked in her chair. "Amy was sent away because she kissed a spy. Nobody really knows who, no one except Dustin Sparks. He's the one who sent her away." The four all looked shocked.

"Why would he do that?!" Isaac asked almost in an angry sort of voice.

"Well, because he didn't apparently like the spy." B's answered uncertainly, "That's all I know."

Max shook his head in amazement as he rubbed his stomach. "How much did we miss?"

B's laughed hard. "Enough to miss fifteen years, I can tell you that!"
As she saw the four stand up, she exclaimed, "Are you leaving already?" they nodded.

"We must but I expect we'll see each other very soon." Levi replied.

"Thank you for your hospitality." Samantha said as she opened the door.

"Anytime dears! Take care of yourselves!" she called as the four wandered away into the woods again. After they left, B's snapped her fingers and the remaining cakes vanished.

~

The four walked through Grandly Forest until dark, then cleared away a spot to make a camp for the night. Isaac slipped out his pillow from his cloak from England when they escaped. The others used their arms. Just as they were getting settled in as they listened to the nighttime commotion.

All was peaceful. Until...
"Sa-man-tha..."

Something whispered. Samantha, startled, oddly sat up. As she looked around, she then shrugged. "Maybe it's just the wind." she rolled over.

"Sa-man-tha..." It whispered again.

Samantha sat up and threw leaves at Max who yelled and sat up, looked around.

"Who's trying to scare me?!" she demanded, as they glared at her.

"Not me!" Levi said hotly as he started to lay down

again. Then the voice came back.

"I know you all think you can hide... you think your brave enough to fight, but I'll tell you something, you'll end up just like your mummy and daddy did... when they thought the same thing!" the voice then died away after that and left an echo with it.

The four looked nervously at each other. Samantha shook her head nervously after a long pause.

"Let's just all go back to bed, and pretend that never happened." she suggested, laying back down.

The boys all nodded and did the same thing. But once everything was quiet again, Samantha couldn't get the scary voice out of her head.

Chapter 8

Chetan

The next morning, the four were still shaken from the voice they had heard the night before. But, they quickly forgot about that when they saw the huge plains in front of them. Isaac packed his pillow up in his large cloak pocket and started off after the others.

The plains were dry but beautiful as the sun rose high and the hills sparkled with tall prairie grass. Isaac studied the map they were following and noticed something. They were headed toward the Sioux village. He knew this because the symbol was in the plains on the map.

He was about to say something when Max said, "Stop!"

Just when the others were about to question him, they stopped too. The ground started rumbling and there was a jarring vibration that shook everyone like crazy.

Levi looked at the hills to see signs and there were. A few brown cows with curved horns and large bumps on their backs came charging down the hill making loud, grunting noises. But now, there were dozens of them. The group grew larger and larger as they ran down the hill.

"Buffalo..." Samantha mumbled.

But there was one major problem, they were headed directly for the four.

"Run!" Max shouted over the loud noise.

They ran for a few dry bushes and dogwood trees and tried to stay as low as possible. The sight of all the buffalo was frightening, yet amazing! There were at least seven hundred beasts charging past them in a huge cloud of dust. They grunted as they ran, their hooves beating almost rhythmically against the dry earth. The four saw several calves trying to keep up with the herd, despite their small stature.

When the stampede was almost over, Levi pulled up to a crouch. Finally, when the last buffalo raced out into the plains, Levi stood up and left the hiding place.

"Levi, get back down!!!" Samantha shrilled.

Just above them, a lone buffalo appeared. The buffalo may have fallen behind the pack that moved into the prairie. Levi wasn't looking and didn't see the danger. Samantha pointed to the hill where the buffalo was running and nearing where the four sought refuge. The beast locked eyes with Levi. Levi stood frozen; hoping the buffalo wouldn't notice him. Unfortunately, it did.

The huge buffalo kicked back it's hooves then a second later, it charged. Levi's eyes went wide. He couldn't look at his siblings – he kept his eyes fixed on the charging buffalo. Closer and closer the buffalo came, kicking up a ball of dust and dirt as it charged.

Out of nowhere, a miracle happened. An arrow shot out only moments before the buffalo would have trampled him. The arrow made a clean shot, directly into the forehead, immediately knocking the beat to the ground. Almost immediately, the buffalo took it last gasp of air as it slipped into a permanent sleep.

Levi couldn't move. Still frozen, the cloud of dust the fallen buffalo had made blinded him. Silence fell; and there was a long terrifying stillness. Levi turned to Isaac, Max and Samantha. They looked just as frightened as he did.

Then, the four heard a small rustling sound coming from a section of the long prairie grass. They all turned to the source of the sound and saw a boy slowly approaching them. He had deer hide clothing, long black silky hair with two braids in the front, framing his tan face. His skin was dark and his eyes were a light brown color.

The boy looked over the dead buffalo than back at the four.

"Were you hunting this buffalo?" he asked.

Levi looked away from the buffalo and to the Indian boy now beside him and his siblings.

"N-No, you can have it." Levi nervously said shaking his head from side-to-side.

The Indian boy smiled. Before he could go over to the buffalo, Levi asked,

"You-speak English?"

The Indian boy nodded. Levi looked again at the others who watched the Indian unblinkingly.

"What's your name?" Levi asked more confidently. The Indian boy paused for a moment, then put his hand to his chest and answered, "Chetan". He looked at all four of the children who stood there frozen like statutes.

"You, your names?" Chetan asked. Levi was beginning to get annoyed that the others were not responding; not even Samantha.

"This is Isaac, Max and Samantha and I'm Levi." he said pointing to his sibling and then himself.

"We are the -er- Four Wonders," he said, almost uncertainly. Chetan's eyes grew wide.

"You are the four?" he asked. "You are the people Dustin Sparks speaks of?"

"Yes." Samantha replied.

Chetan almost chuckled. "I didn't think you were the four because you were so dirty."

Samantha looked embarrassed.

"Come," Chetan said as he began to walk the way he came from.

"Where are we going?" Levi asked.

Chetan replied, "The Sioux people, my people...my village."

Chapter 9

The Different Point Of View

The four tried to keep up while Chetan rode his horse. He seemed to feel sorry that he didn't offer to let the four go on, but it was for the best. The four wouldn't be able to fit. Plus, they were used to walking everywhere. Chetan slowed a bit and said "We are here."

He pointed to a few tepees in the distance which almost looked like cones sticking out of the earth. As they got closer, it became apparent that it was a whole Indian village. Smoke rose from the center of almost every tepee and it smelled like a camp. Entering the village, Chetan slid off his horse and walked with the four through the village.

Two braves came over to retrieve the horse and as they did so, glared at the four.

"Maybe they just don't know it's us." Samantha whispered as they all looked around in amazement.

Chetan led them to an area with mats and tall stacks of blankets. "Wait here." he ordered. He walked away swiftly to a tepee across from them. The four looked around where they stood. It was an amazing sight. Dozens of dark horses were tied to dogwood trees around camp and made a little noise every few seconds. The noises could have been annoying, but didn't seem to bother the Indians at all. They must have grown used to it.

Children raced around the village, laughing and squealing. Some of them stopped to stare at the four. Women, (the ones that weren't staring at them) were mending baskets and hanging meat on wooded racks.

A few of the Indians were chatting in Sioux and the four wished they could understand. It all was so happy and peaceful. Despite this, the four did not feel welcome.

Four women exited the tepee that Chetan went into with large knives, headed towards the plains.

"What are they doing?" Samantha asked in a inquisitive voice.

"They're going out to cut the meat from the buffalo that Chetan had killed." Levi answered abruptly.

"How do you know?" Max asked.

"I read about it." Levi replied.

Isaac looked a bit stunned by this. "You read?!?" Isaac said smirking.

Levi nudged him in the gut. Chetan was not out yet. All appeared well, except they saw an angry Indian girl coming from an diagonal tepee. She had a fierce look on her face; although she was very beautiful. One of the most naturally beautiful girls the four had ever seen. Nonetheless, the four did not fancy her bad attitude at all.

Before anyone could react, the angry girl threw Max and Samantha down on the hard, dry grass. And, soon enough Levi and Isaac were also thrown down right next to them. The girl began kicking them and shouting words they did not understand. Snot and spit flying, she seemed to be cursing at them (although they really didn't know for sure).

Other Indian girls came and also joined in the fight, throwing grass and handfuls of dirt on the four laying on the ground. It was blinding and downright uncomfortable! The boys did not dare to raise their hands to the Indian girls for fear of what might happen to them. Instead they ate dirt. Luckily, Chetan emerged from the tepee and ran towards them. He dropped the bundles of furs he was carrying as he went and ran towards the angry mob of girls.

Chetan roughly grabbed the angry Indian girl and restrained her, holding her arms behind her back. "Stop that!" Chetan shouted as the girl hollered something back in Sioux.
The four remained on the ground, dusty and dirty, looking downward. Chetan scolded the girl, muttering Sioux in her ear. The scolding must have worked since the angry girl quickly walked away. The remaining mob dispersed, leaving the four and Chetan.

All the other Indians were staring wide-eyed at the four. It was humiliating. Having their hair covered in grass and weeds and dirt all over them, they looked homeless, not like the fabled four. Talk about embarrassing.

"What did you tell her?" Levi asked.

Chetan still looked outraged with the girl. "I told her that if she harmed you again, I would be sure that she would be taught a hard lesson." "Luckily for her she is my cousin." "And, I told her you were the four..."

Chetan gave them all clothes made from deer and elk. Once the four were dressed in the clean clothes, Samantha stood at attention. After Chetan walked off, Samantha said to the boys, "Different...very different".

Chapter 10

Buffalo Run

Days with the Sioux were like Samantha said, different. The four had a chance to meet Chief Panamoah. They learned that the girl that had cursed at them was called Enapay. She never cursed at them since the day she had, but that didn't mean that she liked them.

Samantha hated it with the Sioux. She said they're 'uncivil and savage like.' Max well agreed with her. He didn't like Enapay's rude behavior when he tried to act kind to her. Isaac was fond of it. He liked talking to the men, and trying to understand what they were saying. He also liked how they had a sense of humor. They laughed whenever he laughed. But he could see why. Whenever he laughed, his grin would set very wide and he laughed like a barking puppy. No wonder they laughed. They were laughing at *him.*

Levi, however, loved it with the Sioux. He loved almost everything about it. (Despite Enapay...) He also became very close with Chetan. Something happened to the four that never in their lifetime would they forget.

"A buffalo run?" Samantha questioned Chetan as he was stuffing arrows into a quiver.

"Yes." he answered impatiently, "You best get a horse, the men will be leaving soon."

The four left the tepee and went over to the dogwood trees where a dozen horses stood, unmounted.
Levi took a brown and white horse and tried to get on a quick as Chetan did with his pony.
Isaac took a white horse and took his time to mount it. Max and Samantha both boarded both black horses. They kicked to start off their horses within a few steps, they were all following behind Chetan and the young men. The four felt anxious as they rode up hill after hill.

Levi was afraid of becoming embarrassed on this hunt. He didn't want to be. He couldn't fail in front of Chetan, not today. Chetan raised his hand for the riders to stop. Everyone got off their horses and raced for the hill they were going to. Once they were near the top, they all slowed to a creep. They crawled silently and peered over the top. And what they saw, were at least more than five hundred buffalo grazing.

"Washte Tatanka." one brave exclaimed as Chetan nodded.

"What did he say?" Samantha asked.

Levi looked at her and whispered in reply, "He said, 'Good Buffalo.'" the four looked over their shoulders and realized that the braves were already mounting back on their horses. They rushed to catch up and mounted theirs also and realized that they were riding around the hill to attack the buffalo!

Samantha looked petrified. The braves shouted cries and started releasing arrows at the big animals who began grunting and running the other way. Levi rode past a dew braves and chased the fleeing stampede. He aimed for a large buffalo that was trailing quickly and making loud grunts.
He drew back his arm and released an arrow, and he hit it! Right in the leg! The buffalo kept running, limping injured. Levi urged his horse faster as he steadied his bow and released another arrow.
It hit the giant animal in the right lower shoulder.

The buffalo stopped, right away, making noises and looking around, fearfully. Levi circled the buffalo and readied another arrow, let go, and hit the buffalo in the head. It stood frozen for only a second, then it began to lower, until it sank completely to the ground, dead. Levi yelled bravely and ran over to the great beast. He heard Isaac yelling with joy as he ran around a giant buffalo.

Chetan had gotten two, Max got a middle sized buffalo and a calf. (Levi frowned a bit.)
And Samantha, well, she didn't get any. She only sat on her horse looking very hot and pouty. Once the four all met, most of them were happy, (Except Samantha...)

They all laughed with relief. But just then, Isaac's smile wiped off his face and he looked at his cloak. "Why does my cloak feel lighter?" he asked. The others only shrugged. Isaac felt around and he felt his heart sink. "Oh, no,no,no,no,NO!" he cried.

"What's wrong?" Samantha asked in a frantic tone. Isaac looked very upset.

"My pillow! The only thing I have from Amy, it's gone! It must have slipped out!" he looked around at the hills.

"Let's go look for it!" Max suggested. Isaac looked down, disappointed.

"No, there's nothing we can do now... besides, the men are leaving."

Sadly, they slipped onto their horses and rode away into the prairie.

Chapter 11

The Fair Trade

That night, there was a celebration feast. Food, music, dancing, laughing, stories. Just like a party, except more mysterious and awesome. There were stews, breads, and drinks with a taste of berries and maple sugar. The music was low, with echoing drums and shaking rattlesnake tails. Indians danced gracefully around the fire.

Chetan was talking with Chief Panamoah, who stood proudly watching his people enjoying themselves.
Meanwhile, the four sat in the grass, eating their stew and enjoying the interesting scene.

"It's really quite fascinating." said Samantha who was never yet so positive about the Sioux.

"Yeah... It's swell..." Isaac responded lowly, picking at his food and sighing.

Samantha smiled weakly, "It's alright, we'll find your pillow some how."

Max patted Isaac heartily on the back. "Yeah, don't be so hard on yourself." he said.

Isaac pushed his bowl away and looked around at all the Indians. Just then, a look of anger came on his face as his jaw dropped.

"What?" Max asked. Isaac felt outraged.

"That Indian over there... he- he has my pillow!" he said furiously, pointing across the fire. Past the Indians dancing, was a group of young men, and one was holding his pillow, smiling. He was smiling as if he had taken complete possession in it. Him and the other men around him were grinning broadly and whispering. Samantha pulled a dirty look at him. Isaac got to his feet and walked stiffly over to them. They all looked up, some weren't smiling anymore.

"Excuse me, that's mine." he tried telling the one who had his pillow. The brave stared blankly at him. Isaac tried repeatedly, "That pillow is mine." all the men stared at him, unable to understand. Isaac groaned and pointed to the pillow, My-pillow- please-give-back." he said slowly and clearly. And when the warrior still didn't respond, anger boiled in Isaac's blood and he shouted,

"GIVE THAT BACK IT'S MINE!!!" he yelled.

He stopped. He knew he shouldn't have yelled.
Because now, something was different,

No singing.
No dancing.
No music.

Everyone was looking at him. The warrior slowly
got to his feet. He looked very angry. So angry in
fact that he began to raise his fist. But then, Chetan
came running through the staring crowd and spoke
quickly to the warrior. The brave still looked angry.
Chetan turned to Isaac after the warrior spoke.

"He says he'll trade with you." Chetan told him.
Isaac was looking around. He had nothing to trade
for his pillow. But then, it hit him. He quickly went
over to the spot where his rabbit skin bag was and
he took the pin that said 'United We Stand' in gold
letters. He ran back over to where the warrior stood
and held out the pin to him.

He was ready to be laughed at. But instead the
warriors eyes lit up as he quickly handed Isaac his

pillow and took the pin. The warrior held out his tan hand.

"Washtae." he bellowed.

Isaac shook his hand.

"Good- I mean... *Washte.*"

Chapter 12

Trailing Voice

After the trade with the warrior, Isaac became very popular in the Sioux Village. Almost as popular as Levi. But the pride of people constantly smiling at him, and being honored only lasted three days. Because something happened that changed everything.

Chetan and Levi were sitting near the totem poles, playing a game that Levi had never played before while Isaac helped the men make spears, and Samantha and Enapay weaved baskets.
When all of the sudden, the nice white clouds slowly turned black and thunder sounded from far away. And everyone looked up. Isaac's stomach turned to a knot. He had a horrible feeling about who it was.
A neon green mist came from nowhere and trailed around the village leading a deadly voice with it.

"I know why you're here, you think you can defeat me and find Dustin Sparks to help you to it! And you redskins think you can protect the four from

me, But you don't have the powers I have! I can destroy you in a mere second! I destroyed Lindy VerBeek and I sought to destroy her children as well! You four think you can be the heroes your mummy and daddy wanted you to be... But the only hero here is the hero who will be known as the one who finally killed the four and will be the best in the world! If anyone doubts me, I will destroy them as well! Death to all who protect the Four Wonders!!!"

There was a long yell and the mist vanished, along with the dark clouds and everything was back to normal. The people looked at each other in horror. Isaac stood up.

"We'll go then." The others stood up too and began to walk when Chetan stopped them.

"No! It's too dangerous! What will we do when we soon find out that the four were slaughtered by an evil spirit?!"

Max shook his head as he packed his uniform in a deerskin bag. "All must take a dare or two in life."

Levi looked at him oddly. "Since when did you become a poet?" he asked awkwardly.

"I don't know!" he answered hysterically.

Levi rolled his eyes. When they were ready, Chief Panamoah sent them away with a horse for each of them, and buffalo hide blankets. The four then strapped their blankets onto their new ponies, thanked the Sioux, (Levi and Chetan said goodbye to each other...) Then, they rode away.

"Where did you get that?" Max asked Levi, pointing to a new knife as they rode on through the plains. Levi smiled proudly.

"Chetan gave it to me."

Max looked forward. "I wish I had a knife..." he muttered jealously.
Samantha seemed cross. "We have fine blankets and ponies, and Levi only got an extra gift because he's the Sioux's little prince!"

Levi glared at her, "You're just jealous that I got more respect from the Sioux than you did!" he raised his voice.

Samantha seemed deeply offended."Jealous? Of what?! Nothing's fun with them!"

Levi's scowl deepened. "That's because you failed at everything!"

Samantha rode away, beginning to cry.

"Oh you dumb son of a mop, you hurt her feelings!" Isaac scolded.

So the three boys rode ahead after Samantha.

~

"Sam!" Max called as Samantha rode ahead, ignoring them.

"Samantha!" Levi called for the eighth time.

"Samantha, stop!!!" Isaac hollered. Thinking that it was pointless, Samantha finally came to a stop.

"That worked." said Isaac, relived. The boys rode to where Samantha sat frozen solid.

"What's the matter?" Levi asked. Samantha pointed a shaky finger at a jungle.

"What the- It's just a-" Levi's voice died away. They heard something. It sounded like singing. Silently, the four rode toward the jungle and listened until they could finally understand what the voices were saying. It sounded like a very gory song. But they jumped when Max said,

"Look, a cove!"

And indeed there was a cove. Hidden under strands of vines and the four tied their ponies to some trees and peeked through a crack in the mountainous cove wall.

They then listened to the horrid song that the voices sang.

> *"The hoards of horrors,*
> *The plank and borders,*
> *are pirates at the sea..."*

"Pirates..." Max whispered, sounding fascinated.

"Disgusting!!!" Samantha said under her breath, "Their songs don't even make sense!"

"Let's get a closer look." Isaac suggested.

They crept into the cove and hid behind giant, sharp black rocks and crouched into the shallow water.

"We cannot let them see, or hear us." Max whispered.

Samantha didn't like the feeling of wet clothes sticking to her body like flypaper. Especially if the water was cold. The whole ship was in view now and it sent shivers up the fours spines.

Max looked up and saw the Pirates Cove symbol on their flag. Two skulls on each end of a looping rope. And the whole ship was glistening in the morning light, even though it was inside the dark cave. Max crept a little closer, keeping his eyes on the ship at all times. But just as he looked around the corner, he winced.

There was a skeleton with torn, rotted clothes and a black eye patch. He could now hear the clutter of swords being slashed. But then, he had a brilliant idea.

"Guys, come here!" he whispered excitedly. Levi, Isaac and Samantha all nervously crept forward.

"What if the pirates are heading to Wizard Land?" Max murmured.

"Why would they?" Samantha asked bitterly, trying to straighten her wet clothes and looked disgustingly at the ship.

"Well, they could!" Max insisted in a hushed sort of whisper.

Levi hesitated.

"It's a gamble..." he mumbled. Max shook his head.

"It's a chance." he whispered. He looked at the flag bravely, "I'm gonna find out."

Samantha grabbed his arm before he could creep forward.

"Max! No way! They'll beat you to death!" she said in an alarming whisper.

Max huffed annoyingly, "What choice do I have? We need to speak to Dustin Sparks!"

"There is a way..." Isaac began, which hushed the twins. Isaac leaned forward, "We are gonna disguise Max as a pirate, so he can ask them!"

"Alright..." said Max, sounding fine with the idea.

Though Levi and Samantha didn't.

"And how are we going to necessarily do that?!" Samantha asked in a frustrated tone.

Max smiled and pointed to the withered skeleton around the corner of the rocks. After a long silence, the others nodded. As Max slid forward, he felt the muck stick to his shirt and once he was face to face with the skull, he noticed that his clothes were a greenish black. Max tried to take the skeletons clothes without a sound within the process, and it nearly worked. So once he had the smelly white shirt on and a red bandanna around his forehead, (He had to keep on his English breeches...) he grabbed handfuls of muck and smeared it over the front of his shirt to make himself even dirtier. As he tried to swim quietly back, he listened irritably to the pirates singing.

"We'll kill ourselves a dwarf or elf if we please, We'll sort them from short to tall, and then we'll kill them all!"

Once Max made it back to the others, he felt more than proud of himself. Now, he needed to dress the other three up.

Chapter 13

Captain E. Smith

Max decided he would go on the pirate ship to see whether if they were going to Wizard Land or not. If they were, he'd sneak some clothes from the ship and somehow get back to the other three. So, he pretended to be walking on one leg as he entered the dock. (He had climbed up the ladder dangling at the side of the ship...)

He observed all the pirates as they worked. Mel was right. They surely did wear shiny bling. Now, Max felt stupid. He wished he had some bling. A few girls were on the ship too, except they were as ugly as a devil. They had way too much makeup on, their lips were coated in red lipstick not to mention bulgy.
Their hair was puffy, or madly curled, and they had the worst teeth.

Then, Max shuttered. Upon the staircase, was a tall, thick man with a peg leg and a blue jacket with black leggings and boots, his jacket had gold buttons and epaulets with tassels, exactly like Isaac's pillow. A huge gold chain with a shiny red stone shown proudly on his chest. On his head sat a giant black pirates hat with a skull on the front. He must be the captain.

He cleared his throat, most of the pirates looked up, that meaning everyone but the crushed skeletons lying on the floor.

"Well, sing the anthem!" he bellowed.
The pirates all jumped, startled, and began to sing.

"Our Captain E. Smith, the ruler of the seven savage seas,
He rides the whales as some would say, but he really cuts em' gory.
Oh Captain E. Smith, King of coves, and wherever he goes,
He'll say good bye, and don't ye cry,
He'll cut you up in four..."

Then, everyone cheered as the captain bowed as though he had sung it himself. Max had pretended to sing but near the end, he was too nervous to keep going. Now came the 'best' part. A pirate nudged him in the shoulder, and he jerked around.

"Good 'ol captain aye mate?" he said heartily. Max tried to deepen his voice.

"Yeah..." he bellowed. Then, he remembered, "Where are we going?"

The pirate seemed shocked.

"To our treasure spot 'o course!" he replied.

"And where exactly is that?" Max asked.

"By Wizard Land, stupid!" the pirate shouted, as he walked away.

Max smirked. Now he just needed clothes for the other three.

~

When nobody was looking, Max jumped off the edge of the boat and into the water and swam deep down until his chin hit the sand. He peered up and saw Isaac, Levi and Samantha and swam to them.

"They're headed for Wizard Land!" Max said when he made it to them. Isaac grinned.

"Good! Now we need to disguise ourselves." Isaac frowned as he looked from Levi, to Samantha, then himself. Max grinned and he pointed to a window near the bottom of the ship.

"There are clothes in there." he said. Levi looked over to where he was pointing.

"How do you know?" Max's grin broadened.

"Because I saw some pirate gals heading toward some double doors when one said, 'I need another dress. Let's go downstairs and get one.'"

Max frowned, "I just hope it's the right window..."

Samantha seemed to be thinking, but then she said, "Alright, let's go!" and they began to swim for the window. They swam deep below the surface until they could barely see anything. Max could see the shadows of his siblings swimming behind on the silver like sand.

They finally reached the window and Isaac peered through the dirty glass. And sure enough, there were clothes. There was a right orange dress hanging up in an open closet, followed by pink, purple, green, blue and yellow dresses. There were several black uniforms and white shirts with lace on the sleeves and a row of magnificent black pirates hats.

Max dove underwater again and came back up with a sea rock. He looked through the room window to make sure there was going to be nobody else except them. Fortunately, there wasn't anyone. So like a hammer, he smashed in the window. Luckily, it shattered very fast and Max kept on smashing until he and his siblings were able to get in.

One by one, they entered the room, and hastily got dressed. Isaac and Levi both put on white laced shirts and tied black and red bandannas to their heads, Isaac's red, Levi's black. Samantha threw on a blue dress and messed up her blonde hair to make it look somewhat frizzy. Then, she fastened black, shoes that pinched her toes and looked in the window to see her reflection. The boys were now ready also.

They all looked at one another. They knew that hey had to leave the horses behind. They even hid their deerskin bags stuffed away inside their shirts and

Samantha hid hers under her skirt. Isaac hid his pillow in one of the chests and hoped he'd remember it.

Finally they were ready. They shuffled up the wooden stairs and tried to blend in with the rough characters.

Chapter 14

Red and Blue

"May I have yer attention?" Captain Smith called. All the pirates looked up from what they were doing and the four tried to mimic their ugly stares. Samantha stood impatiently by the group of gals Max had seen. The captain seemed just as impatient as Samantha.

"We'll begin sailing as soon as ye all shut yer gulls!!!" all the pirates remained silent. Captain Smith grinned, "Good!" he slapped the rail and within seconds later, the ship began to move. Everyone quickly went back to what they were doing before.

"They could do better cleaning the floor if there weren't so many skull bones everywhere." Max mumbled to himself as he watched some pirates sweep away piles of dust. Max then turned around and shivered. A pirate with one eye (The other covered with an eye patch...) and rotten teeth and slick blonde hair came to him. Max looked behind himself wishing that the pirate was going to talk to someone else. He did like the little Capuchin monkey sitting on the pirates shoulder.

"H'lo mate! Name's Squint! Cappin's assistant. Do ye have any tobacco?" he asked. Max stared, unable to speak.

"I- I don't think so sir..." Squint shrugged and grinned.

"Aye!" he bid him goodbye and walked away.

Max watched him as he walked away. Such a kind soul for such an ugly face. All of the sudden, Max heard something. Sounds of swords crashing together broke through. Two pirates were sword fighting and cursing at each other. The first pirate wore red and black and the second pirate wore blue and black. Max decided to name them "Red and Blue".

Red swung his sword hard and Blue blocked it with his. The cussing, the slashing seemed to go on forever. The altercation grew more serious. Red tried to stab Blue in the chest, but missed and fell into some beer barrels. Blue raised his sword, but Red was back on his feet and swiping back and forth with his sword. Then, Blue tripped Red over who fell helplessly down. But surprisingly, Red hadn't given up. Because he reached out and stabbed Blue hard in the stomach. He let out a high pitched gasp and fell to the ground, dead. The pirates cheered on and on and slapped Red in the back to congratulate him. A lone pirate came over with a rope and tied it around Blue's waist. And he threw him into the ocean and held onto the rope tight.

Max looked over and saw that Squint was standing next to him and whispered, "What is he doing?"

Squint let out a small laugh. "He'll make good fish grub." he answered, smirking.

Samantha looked disgusted and ran over to Max. "This place is horrible!" she whispered soberly.

Max shushed her and turned back to Squint. "I think I'll go take a nap." he said. But before he could go, Squint stopped him.

"We're about to go have some rum! C'mon!" he cheered, as he and the other pirates rushed down the creaky stairs.

Samantha and the other girls stood there, talking. It looked like Samantha was doing alright, so Max followed Squint and the men into the candle lit dining room. Tables and benches were spotted here and there, but Max and Squint sat by the bar. He felt sort of nervous. He never had beer before, plus he was underage. A chubby pirate handed him a tall, dusty glass which contained golden colored beer. Max drank away and after awhile, his stomach began to hurt very bad. He wished he was sitting with Isaac and Levi at the table in the corner, because Squint was talking his bloody ear off.

But finally around midnight, they all slept in hammocks, and out of all the snoring, Max luckily found sleep and sleep found Max.

Chapter 15

The Serpents Bait

Max and Levi were walking along the dock, admiring the gorgeous day and how well the sea sparkled. Isaac and a few pirates were sharpening swords while Samantha was learning the girls names. Helga, Olga, Sasha, and Antoinette. They were twirling around the floor. Max leaned on a beam and grinned.

"What are you smiling at?" Levi asked. Max chuckled a bit.

"I'm thinking about what Blue would look like by now..." Levi slowly smiled.

"Let's find out." he said quietly. The boys raced across the dock and looked over the boat and saw Blue, dead skin and foam around his drifting body.

"Lays like a log don' he?" the pirate watching him

said sarcastically. Max nodded while Levi kept on flinching while staring at Blue. Then, he noticed something different. The sky wasn't nice anymore.

Max felt the urge to think that it was Dietomorse, but no. The clouds looked like storm clouds.

"Looks like a storms a growin..." observed the pirate.

Then, he looked around while Max and Levi focused back on Blue. Max looked behind him and saw Squint talking with another pirate and observing a pearl necklace. Max hid his face by turning back to Levi. But he looked even stranger. He was looking horrifyingly at Blue.

"What?" Max asked, concerned. Levi stuttered,

"I- I see something..." Max looked down at the water closely. Before he had a chance to ask Levi what he saw, the whole ship rocked. Max and Levi hung onto the beam. Then, they looked to see if Isaac and Samantha were alright. They were. Then Max remembered, Blue. They looked down and saw that Blue was still there. But as the boys looked closer, they aw something floating upward from beneath him. It looked like a monstrous head. And it came closer. Levi only blinked once before it shot out of the water, swallowing Blue whole and pulling the man with the rope underwater, drowning him.

A light green, glistening creature swam up and hissed loudly, showing its large and long pointy teeth. It dived back down and the boat rocked several times, showering water all over the ship. People fell over top of each other and landed on the plank floor in a single bang. The green creature shot out of the water once again and dove majestically over the pirate ship.

Captain Smith came hurrying out of his private room, apparently he looked like everyone else except instead his hair was askew and not soaked like the other his hat had fallen, revealing a pink bald patch on his head.

"Sea serpent!!!" he shouted loudly, "Gather your weapons!!!" he shouted over the roaring beast.

People were screaming and clutching onto each other and any beams and door handles they could find. Max and Levi tried to run to Isaac and Samantha but fell back by the smash of the serpents body they crashed into some crates which were falling overboard. The serpents grip increased and the floor boards began to groan and crack. The serpent sank its fangs into the crows nest and the lookout fell with a single shout. The boat was nearly split in half!

Max hung onto Levi's arm as the serpent plainly destroyed the ship. Both boys sighed with relief when they saw Isaac and Samantha running toward them.

"This is crazy, we have to jump!!!" Max said to them. Samantha looked frightened; same for Isaac.

"But how are we going to get to Wizard Land?!" Isaac asked. Levi shouted over the serpents hissing and high screams.

"Captain Smith said about another three miles to go!!!"

The four all nodded and Max counted to three.

"One...Two...Three!!!"

And with that, the four plunged into the turbulent waters.

Chapter 16

The Secret Ride

"I hope the serpent doesn't get our scent..." said Samantha in a worried voice as they swam through the ocean waters.

"Looks like he's too busy destroying the ship." Levi observed in the distance. They saw several rescue boats rowing the other way. Max could hear Squint shout, 'Where's that lad, Max?!" he heard him say.

Max sighed sadly. "Well at least Squint's on the rescue ship and safe." Isaac glared at him.

"We should've gone with them!" Samantha glared back at Isaac.

"They're not going to Wizard Land! They're going in the opposite direction!!!" she said through clenched teeth. Max nodded. The sun was beginning to go down. The four at least had another hour.

"We need to keep going..." Levi said bossily. Samantha splashed with a kick and went underwater.

"What is she doing?" Isaac asked Max, who shrugged.

A few moments later, she came up gasping for air. "I don't see anything!" she breathlessly gasped.

"What are you looking for?" Isaac asked.

Samantha shrugged and answered quietly, "I may or may not have stolen a few shells off the pirate ship, and now I've lost them!"

Levi groaned. "Why would you take something off the ship?"

Samantha gave a pouty look. "They were pretty shells, and I wanted a couple to show Amy for when we get home." Then, she looked out at the never ending sea. "Do you think we'll ever find Wizard Land?" she asked.

Max looked down and shrugged again.

Isaac was looking dully at the bottomless sea.

"What's the matter?" Levi asked. Isaac sighed and looked at him sadly.

"My pillow... I left it... on the ship..."

Samantha looked at him and put a hand on his shoulder as they kicked in position.

"I'm sorry." she said quietly. Levi was about to say something, but instead he looked upset.

"Are you kicking me?" he demanded to Isaac, who shook his head defensively.

"Nope." he answered. Levi now looked panicky.

"There's something under me!" Isaac looked down into the deep, dark ocean.

"I don't see anything, Levi! Let's just concentrate on getting back to shore!"

But before they could all start swimming again, Samantha screamed and plopped underwater.

"Samantha!!!" The boys cried.

Then, Levi plopped under too. Isaac tried looking to see where they were going, but in about a second, he was underwater too. Max was screaming his head off.

He looked through the water and popped up every few seconds for air. Nothing.
But just then, he felt himself being dragged down underwater too. He thought he was drowning and so he frantically tried freeing himself from the tight grasp of his ankle. But whoever was pulling on him, kept dragging him and never loosened grip. Max thought he'd stop breathing in any second, and when he was going to start fighting with his hands, he took a long good look at them. They were webbed, and same for his feet. He touched his face and felt something strange on his neck, it had gills. He tried to see who was pulling on his leg and dragging him through the ocean, and when he saw what it was, he couldn't believe his eyes.

It was a girl with gills on her neck, a tail like a fish, and long tangled black hair with white shells scattered about the locks. She was as pale as the moon, and her tail was bright blue.

"Mermaids." Max exclaimed with bubbles exploding from his mouth.

He said 'mermaids' because there was more than one. He saw that his siblings were being dragged through the ocean by mermaids too. As the mermaids dragged them through the ocean, Max noticed that they were going through a coral reef. Bright coral was around and looking shimmery and beautiful. Except this coral reef was giant and Max noticed that mermaids were living inside the coral. It was a mere-people village. There was also tall seaweed. Max had a whole bunch brush up against him. He saw families of mere-people. An old merman waved to the girl dragging Max and she nodded in reply. He saw a mother mermaid with her baby swim past him. Schools of fish glided about the village and glimmered in the sparkling surface above.

Now, as they left the coral reef, he saw sand now, and realized they were near land. The mermaid let go. She was beautiful.

"Your majesties..." she whispered in a bow. And then, she swam away. Max now felt like he was suffocating because he no longer had gills. He swam to shore and met his siblings there.

"What in God's name was that?! Those beautiful

lady fish things lead us away from Forever Land!"
Isaac cried.

Samantha shook her head and rolled her eyes.

"Even though we lost the map, I remember seeing
the Island split up into several parts. It was
amazing!"

Max looked even more grouchy than Isaac.

"We lost our map?!"

Samantha nodded. Levi didn't pay attention,
instead, he said,

"No... The mermaids... they gave us rides... we're in
Wizard Land..."

Chapter 17

The Guard

Wizard Land was a place like unlike anything they had ever seen. The buildings and houses were tall and so beautiful in the starry night. The four could see tall lampposts with golden streamers lined around the street. It all looked so nice, even though the four weren't inside yet.

A big iron gate stood in front of them that said 'Wizard Land.' All of the sudden, bagpipes and an Irish flute were sounded and the four could hear people shouting. With no warning, fireworks exploded and showered the night sky. There were purple letters that said in in showering sparks,

Dustin Sparks Rules

People cheered on and on. There must have been more than ten thousand people cheering. But that didn't matter to the four.

"Dustin Sparks is here! We can finally talk to him about how to defeat Dietomorse!" Isaac exclaimed, running for the gate.

The other three followed him. But before he could open the gate, a guard came out of nowhere and held his long sword high. He was a large, bulging man.

"Password?" he demanded. The four looked at one another, stunned.

"Recomarano?" Samantha guessed.

"NO!!!" the guard shouted.

"Dustin Sparks?" Levi tried.

"NO!" the guard hollered. Isaac smirked a bit.

"Wizard pie?" he tried hopefully.

"NO! But I do love Wizard pie." he responded.

"Guards rule over people?" said Max.

"NO, NO, NO!!! But they should..." the guard said

back. Samantha tried one more time.

"The Four Wonders?" she tried hopelessly.

"NO!!!" The guard rubbed his eyes. They sighed.

"Let's go..." said Samantha, discouraged, "Even us, the Four Wonders can't go in."

And with that, they slowly walked away.

"WAIT!!!" the guard called. The four turned around. The guard looked at them hopefully. "Did you say... Four Wonders?" he exclaimed. Samantha nodded. The guard seemed furious with himself.

"By thunder why didn't ye say so?!" he raised his sword.

"Open the gate!"

With that, the gates slowly moaned opened. The guard swept his arm out in a friendly sort of way to let the four in properly. The other guards all bowed down as they each passed. As soon as they entered the city, they could stand still, breathless. Tiki torches lit the cobblestone street and the four saw markets, hotels, bars, cafes, stores and houses were lined down the stretching street. In the center of the block, was a large fountain. Crowds of people were singing, dancing and laughing.

"It's so wonderful!" Samantha exclaimed.

"This is perfect!" Max said happily.

"This has got to be my favorite place!" said Isaac joyfully over the music.

Levi would have said something, but he was too busy dancing with some wizard girls.

"I'll fetch him..." Isaac assured them as he entered the circle of pretty dancing wizard girls and grabbed Levi by the arm and brought him back while the girls groaned but then quickly went back to dancing.

"What are you doing?!" Levi shouted.

"Don't you see you dumb git? These streets are filled! Stay by us!" Isaac scolded him.

Then, a small child stepped out and cried, "Look everybody, it's the Four Wonders!" she squealed with delight. That's when it happened. Soon enough, everyone was looking at them after people quieted others down. Silence fell over everyone.

Samantha drew her wet hair behind her ears and Isaac pushed his glasses into place. Max brushed seaweed from his shirt and Levi looked from side to side. A short man, with brown hair and a brown mustache and had spectacles, pushed his way through the crowd. He stopped and stood diagonally from the four. He removed his spectacles and said,

"Your greatness's, Dustin Sparks has been waiting for your arrival."

Chapter 18

Dustin Sparks

Everyone in the city then wanted to hug, shake hands and speak with the four. The short man pushed his way through the crowds of screaming and cheering wizards and let the four follow close behind.

Finally they reached a long stone bridge that stretched out into the water, and lead to a huge tower. They ran over to it and two knights closed the bridge gate. Now it was finally quiet once again and the noises were far away. After ten minutes, thy weren't even half way across the bridge. But thankfully, the small man broke the awkward silence.

"My name is Mr. Jubini Mangoleo the great Dustin Sparks' personal assistant." he said as he waddled down the bridge in front of the four. He quickly turned around,

"Why, I must know your names! I simply cannot say I met the Four Wonders but never knew their names!" Samantha smiled.

"I'm Samantha VerBeek, and this is Isaac, Levi and Max." she said pointing to each boy, who waved. Mr. Mangoleo smiled his mustache.

"Pleasure!" he cheerfully said as he began walking again.

Now, they were almost at the tower. It was, of course, bigger than what it was in the distance. Mr. Mangoleo reached for the brass door handle and quietly opened it. And when the four saw the inside, it was a long hallway with torches flickering and long tapestries hanging on the walls. Red, plush carpet covered most of the floor and Mr. Mangoleo led them down the grand hall. They passed several doors, large staircases and statues. Samantha glanced at one of the tapestries, and she could remember from the map of what it was. It was a tapestry of the Wizard Land symbol. A large silver circle with a cross in the center and three rings tying around it in loops.

Soon, the four entered a dark room, with a single staircase and only two torches. Mr. Mangoleo pointed to a double spruce wood door at the top of the staircase.

"He's in there." he said, "He's been in there for days." and then, he waddled away.

The four looked at each other.

"Let's go then..." Samantha mumbled. Step by step, they went up the stairs. A cold shiver went up Samantha's spine as they got closer and closer. Just then, a coo-coo clock sounded devilishly. And the four jumped. Isaac reached out slowly and began to turn the knob. It squeaked and they they opened the door, and they walked inside. The room was warm, but dense.

BANG! Something hit Max in the back of the head.

"OW!!!" he cried. His voice echoed throughout the room.

"Who's there?" a low voice called from above.

The four all froze. Upon a small staircase, which appeared to be a balcony of some sort, stood a tall, skinny man. He held his wand high and uttered words that made the room light up. He had fair skin, thick eyebrows, he wore a purple cloak and a tall wizard cap. The four could tell that he had a hairless head, but he had whiskers going from the top of his mouth and spreading out a ways. He was taller than B's, but shorter than Mel.

He had a very long wand. Dustin Sparks.

"Who are you?" he asked. He examined the four from where he was standing. They could see his face flush red and his eyes grow wide.

"Oh my, is this? Can it possibly be?" he slowly came down the stairs. Now that the four could see him perfectly, he was really an impressive sight. But the astonished look on his face gave them a hint that he was clearly amazed.

"You have arrived, Four Wonders." he gasped.

"Fifteen years I've waited, and here you all are." the four were all speechless.

Levi looked around the room and realized what it was now. It was like a colorful library and best of all, there were books that had wings. Flying books! And that was what hit Max in the head.

"Your home is outstanding!" Levi exclaimed.

"Thank you." Dustin Sparks chuckled.

"Do you want us to say our names?" Samantha politely offered. Dustin Sparks held up a hand and shook his head.

"No need. Mr. Mangoleo told me."

Isaac paused from his admiration and gave Dustin Sparks a funny look.

"How did he tell you?" he asked. Dustin Sparks looked at the flying books and answered,

"We talk in our heads." When the four thought he was kidding, but he said he wasn't, the four were bewildered.

"So, Isaac, Levi, Max and Samantha, what have you come for?" he asked curiously.

"Lot's of reasons sir." Isaac answered, "For one thing, how to get to Dietomorse."

Dustin Sparks gave the four a very serious look. But he answered quietly,
"Do you want to get to Dietomorse to kill him?"

"Well not exactly that." Isaac responded, shaking his head. Dustin Sparks smiled.

"You want to meet him because he killed your parents, don't you?"

The four all nodded.

Dustin Sparks looked down, "Well, I know that your idea to meet Dietomorse, won't be easy." his voice sounded dangerous, "He killed your mother because she was the first human to discover magic. And the first to find Forever Land and raise it back on its feet."

"So... Dietomorse was jealous then?" Samantha asked angrily. Dustin Sparks nodded.

"Another thing to know is that he has a temple, that contains a basilisk. We call it Dietomorse's beast. But that's not all, when you reach his temple, there are seven hallways;

1. Cobblestone hallway
2. Grass hallway
3. Plank hallway
4. Marble hallway
5. Glass hallway

6. Granite hallway
7. Alabaster Stone hallway

Now, you will go to my garden in the back of the tower, and find a huge cyan colored crystal. You must touch it and then you will spawn in the Black Forest, right where Dietomorse's temple is."

The four nodded. And Levi asked, "Is there anything in the seven hallways besides the beast?"

Dustin Sparks nodded. "There will be traps or battles in each hallway. And you must go through whatever hall you choose, without turning back. Once you've won your battle, a sign will come and take you into a deserted dome room, you'll be safe inside there until all of you are done with your battles."

"So... We could die then?" Samantha asked nervously.

Dustin Sparks sighed and nodded once more. "But all of Forever Land has faith in you." he answered. He held up a hand before the four could speak again.

"The citizens of Forever Land informed me on

giving you gifts." he said, pulling out a large sack. Now he opened it and pulled out a large tomahawk, with a new buffalo hide belt.

"Levi, this is from Chetan. He wishes you good luck." Levi slowly took the tomahawk and grinned.

"Please tell him that I said thank you." he said gratefully.

"I will." Dustin Sparks promised. Now, he turned to Max. And he pulled out a tooth necklace. Max looked at Levi's tomahawk, then back at his plain tooth necklace. Dustin Sparks chuckled and shook his head.

"Open the tip and let a drop fall out." he directed. Max slowly unscrewed the tip of the shark tooth and let a drop squeeze out from inside. It sparkled blue and formed a dagger on the ground. Max was amazed.

"It's from Squint." said Dustin Sparks.

Max smiled, relived. "So he is alright then?"

Dustin Sparks smiled. "Yes, they built a new ship, and after you arrived at Wizard Land, he soon found out that you were apart of the Four Wonders, and he and Captain Smith want to give you his best."

Max stood, still staring at his gift. "Give him my best too." he said.

Dustin Sparks nodded and then turned to Samantha. He held out a silver wand and book that said,

50 Spells For Young Pupils
It's your magic worth waiting for

Her eyes grew wide as she reached out and slowly took it from Dustin Sparks. He pointed at the wand.

"Try it and see what it does." he smiled. Samantha looked through her book a moment, then pointed her wand at a flying book.

"Blustrado!" she cried and the book smashed to pieces. She then stopped and apologized for destroying Dustin Sparks' book. But he didn't care.

Samantha asked, "Who sent this to me?"

"Mr. Mangoleo." Dustin Sparks answered.

"Is he still here?"

Dustin Sparks shook his head. "He's in the city right now."

Samantha shrugged and smiled. "Tell him I love my gift."

Dustin Sparks smiled. He reached into the red sack and gave Isaac a very wide grin, and he pulled out a long, golden sword and carefully handed it to Isaac. He couldn't believe his eyes as he slowly took it. Dustin Sparks then said,

"This is from me..."

Isaac stammered in return. "Th- Thank you- sir."

With a single nod, Dustin Sparks pointed to the ceiling.

"Slash a book." he ordered. But Isaac didn't want to destroy any of Dustin Sparks' belonging, but he said it was alright. So, Isaac aimed for the lowest flying book and slashed it in half in less than one second. Isaac froze and stood unblinkingly at his sword as the sky turned indigo.

"This was the fastest night of my life!" Levi exclaimed.

Dustin Sparks smiled casually. "Well, today is Tuesday." he said promptly. When he saw that the four didn't understand, he explained.

Sunday is thirty hours total.
Tuesday is five hours total.
Wednesday is twenty five hours total.
Thursday is nineteen hours total.
Friday is twenty nine hours total.
Saturday is thirty one hours total.

"You forgot Monday!" said Max.

Dustin Sparks looked confused. "What is Monday?" he asked.

Max hesitated awkwardly and said, 'never mind.'

"Anyways..." Dustin Sparks changed the subject, "I wish you all good luck on your journey."

"Wait!!!" Isaac called before he could bid them 'good bye.'

Dustin Sparks turned around.

"What is it?" he asked. Isaac took a breath and explained how they needed to know more information about their parents, Amy being sent away, and all the threats from Dietomorse. And after all those questions, Dustin Sparks had only one answer. He took form a shelf, a large crystal ball, it was a ball that a fortune teller would use and a pinky-size beaker that contained a blue acid.

"Go outside my garden gate and pour this inside before you go into the Black Forest and all your questions shall be answered."

"Thank you very much sir." Isaac said. The four left the library with their new weapons.

"Anytime!" Dustin Sparks called after them.

He smiled after the door closed. "Anytime." he whispered to himself.

Chapter 19

The Scary Truth

The four exited out the back door and hurried off in the misty morning over to Dustin Sparks' garden. The garden gate didn't have a guard to ask the password, but the four couldn't go inside just yet.

"He said do it outside the gate." Samantha reminded them.

Max nodded and they crouched down.

"Come on now, Isaac, you have the juice! Stop fiddling with your sword!" Levi ordered.

"Alright, alright!!!" Isaac groaned as he lay his sword down and unscrewed the ball cap.

Then, Max pulled the stopper from the beaker and poured the acid inside. It slid down slowly like molasses and looked so revolting Ma almost threw up. Isaac watched as the blue acid slid all the way to the bottom. And they waited.

~

"Nothing's happening." said Max impatiently five whole minutes later.

"We should just bring the ball back to Dustin Sparks and tell him that it's not working." Levi huffed.

The boys all nodded and stood up.

"Wait!" Samantha called after them.

The boys slowly turned around to see Samantha staring at the ball. The acid was bubbling. The bubbles expanded more and more as the boys scurried to sit down. Then, tiny glittery bubbles popped the big thick bubbles and steam shot out of each hole that it made. Finally, the ball was completely steamed up.

Something formed like a television screen. There was a small, white cottage on a hill. Out came a man and woman. They seemed to be loading a wagon.

"Well now dear, we must make it to the city. Time to kiss the old cottage goodbye!" the man said. He had a very white smile. Same for the woman.

"Now Morris, England is only a few miles away. We'll be fine."

"Right, but Miranda, the children take longer than we do, it could be midnight by the time we reach England city."

Miranda laughed and beckoned to the front door.

"Come along, children." she called.

From the front doorway, came two children, a boy and a girl. Morris lifted another trunk into the wagon.

"Come on now, Clarence, Jennifer, we must hurry." Miranda seemed to be looking around.

"Lindy? Where's Lindy?"

A small girl with beautiful blonde hair and a lovely smile stepped out.

"Here I am, mother!"

Miranda smiled back.

"Into the wagon you go, dear, once we get settled in, we'll see if there's any doctor around who can examine you." she helped Lindy into wagon and then got into the front seat next to her husband, and they were off.

Now, they were in some sort of a doctors office. He was listening to Lindy's heart and nodding.
"Has she been doing anything strange lately?" he asked. Miranda nodded quickly.

"She's been having nightmares and whenever she eats and looks at her food, the dish explodes!" she explained.

The doctor looked from Lindy's curious face, to Miranda's and said, "I don't know what I can do for you, madam. Your daughter is defiantly different. I don't know entirely,

But there could be something." he replied. Miranda looked stressed, but hopeful.

"Oh? What? What is it?" she asked anxiously. The doctor looked down.

"She could be a... *wizard.*" Miranda seemed shocked.

"My daughter's a... what?!"

The doctor nodded. "It's alright, just don't tell anyone."

Then, Lindy was at somewhat of a school, and she was being pushed by three older looking girls.

"You're such a liar! There's no such thing as magic!" one girl said and she pushed her down.

When they walked away, Lindy got up and ran. She kept on running down the halls until she reached the door. She opened it and sat in the grass, crying. She was alone. But just then, a train appeared from nowhere, The F.L express. The train doors opened and there was Mel. Only he wasn't the Mel the four saw on the train when he arrived for them. He looked much younger. He didn't have hair sticking up everywhere, he had a huge beard and still had his buck teeth.

"Welcome aboard!" he cheered, "And what might your name be, little miss?"

Lindy wiped her tears away and said,

"Lindy Eva Quin, what's yours?"

"Mel Kankoff, driver off the F.L express." he said heartily.

Lindy giggled and climbed up the train steps and Mel took off to Forever Land.

Lindy was now dancing with the Sioux Indians, laughing and dancing gracefully around the fire. They treated her like a princess. And now, Lindy was on the pirate ship. And she was sword fighting a small, blonde haired child.

"C'mon, Squint! Come and catch me!" they giggled and fought until they fell onto the floor. The whole crew burst out laughing.

Now, Lindy was in Grandly Forest. She was hugging a small dwarf with a dutch costume.

"Goodbye, B's! Thank you for all your hospitality!"

Lindy called as she walked away.

"Anytime dear!" B's called back.

Finally, Lindy was in Wizard Land shaking hands with Dustin Sparks, (Who looked around the age of twenty.) there were hundreds of people cheering and looking on.

"I crown this fine young lady, Lindy, for raising Forever Land back on its feet! I crown her the chosen one!" he announced and the people cheered on and on. He placed a silver tiara on her head.

And now as Lindy walked down the streets with people reaching out to her, a small girl with black hair and olive skin bumped into Lindy. Both girls fell on their bottoms. The young girl seemed mortified.

"Oh- I- I'm sorry!" Lindy helped the girl up.

"That's alright! Everyone's bound to bump into someone everyone once in awhile! Sometimes literally!" The girl giggled.

"I'm Amy." she said shyly. Lindy grinned.

"I'm Lindy." she responded kindly.

Then, both girls ran off together.

And now what the four saw, were two young women running through the field, laughing and holding hands. They saw a large, beautiful maple tree and ran to it. They fell down and burst out laughing as they watched the leaves fall gently from the tree. Just then, from behind the other side if the large tree, came a man with dark brown hair and a handsome, chiseled face. He carried a smooth broomstick.

"Hello." he said in a friendly tone, "I'm Jack VerBeek. I'm looking for Wizard Land."

Lindy and Amy both quickly stood up. Amy looked at Lindy and smiled the 'you like him' sort of smile.

Lindy ignored the smile and responded, "Well, Jack VerBeek, I'm Lindy Quin, and Wizard Land is that way." she directed, pointing West.

Jack smiled slyly. "Well, do you mind if you take me there yourself?" he asked.

Amy smiled broadly at Lindy who stared at him for

a moment, then, she slowly nodded.

The four then saw Lindy in a beautiful white dress, and Jack in a handsome tuxedo. They kissed. They were married. Lindy now sat in a small home, nice and tidy, but small. She and was playing on the floor with a small boy around two years old.

"Where's mommy, Isaac? Peekaboo!" she said, and the two year old laughed. Lindy turned to a small baby boy in a cradle right next to her.

"Levi's a rare thing, that one." she said, touching his chubby cheek.

When Lindy stood up, the four realized that she was pregnant, with Max and Samantha.
Now, they heard a scream and they saw a dead body on the floor, it was Jack's. Lindy was running outside with two babies under each one, she was fleeing to the field and over to the large maple tree. She hid with all four babies, but then, she heard a shout.

"Chosen one! Come out now!" It was Dietomorse's voice.

Lindy looked sadly at all four of her babies and

whispered, 'I love you.'

And she came out from behind the tree. Dietomorse stood there, his face covered by his black cloak.

"Where are they, Chosen One?"

Lindy shook her head. "Gone" she answered.

Dietomorse stood there, his hand out a her, ready to curse. He shouted,"You have one more chance! Where are they?!" Lindy looked at him bravely and answered,

"Gone. For good."

"Al Jubacabra!!!" Dietomorse shouted, and Lindy was struck dead.

As soon as Dietomorse had left, they saw Amy, sobbing as she lay next to her best friend. She had all four babies next to her as a great storm came.

Then, they saw her in Dustin Sparks' tower and they heard him shouting,

"How dare you kiss a spy! You shall be sent away and never to return!"

Amy only had one thing to say. "I'm taking the four with me then!!!" and she left the tower with that last word.

SHEEYOW!!!

The four woke up on the ground in front of Dustin Sparks' garden gate. Had they fallen asleep? The four couldn't speak to each other. They saw the sun set and they looked at the ball, which was now black as the darkest night.

Chapter 20

Brother Versus Brother

After a long unspeakable moment, the four all broke the silence.

"Whoa! Oh my gosh! That was so weird!!!" Isaac stood up.

"That ball explained everything! Dietomorse, our parents, Amy leaving!!!"

Max stood up too. "Just two more things. Who was the spy, and why Dustin Sparks didn't like him."

Samantha had tears rolling down her cheeks. "Mum... Dad... They died for us." she mumbled with clenched teeth.

"They sacrificed so much..." Levi's voice died away.

"We were b-" Max looked down.

"What was that, Max?" Isaac asked.

Max looked up, he was smiling, but he had tears in his eyes. "We were born in Forever Land..." he said quietly.

"Ever since Amy kissed the spy, Amy took us and raised us as infants, we stayed with her at Iron Gates because we had no one. So that basically makes Amy our- our- our Godmother."

Isaac suddenly glared after hearing that. "She never told us... how dare she! We had to suffer about the place, we had to be treated like slaves! And she never had the decency to purchase a home, or different clothes, and she never even told us that she was practically related to us!"

Max suddenly stepped forward. His face full of fury. "Why did she take us then? Why did she raise us ever since our parents died? Why didn't she buy different clothes or a house, well, maybe she couldn't afford it! But she worked at Iron Gates and gave us a room to sleep in! And why did she save us from Dietomorse that night? Why did she take us to Forever Land in the first place?"

He didn't pay attention to Samantha who was still sitting with tears in her eyes, and Levi watching in horror.

"Because she loves us!" Max hissed.

Everything was silent. Max looked at Isaac, his arms crossed and eyes pierced. Isaac stared at Max his eyes wide with anger and his mouth in a forbidden line. Levi looked at both boys with his eyes wide and kept his mouth shut. Samantha crossed her fingers. Max jerked his head at the gate.

"Come on." he said to Levi and Samantha.

The two got up and followed Max over to the gate.

"Wait!!!" Isaac called. The three turned around. Isaac smirked a bit.

"Wait for me..."

Chapter 21

Seven Hallways

The four raced down Dustin Spark's garden trail which was covered in green leaves, scattered all over the yard. The trail was filled with all sorts of beautiful, healthy plants. It almost looked like a scene straight from a magazine.

Finally, the four saw something shining blue around the corner. The blue crystal. The four all ran for it and when they got close to it, they slowly approached it.

"All we need to do is touch it." Samantha reminded them. They nodded. Isaac turned to face them.

"Look, I know we are all tired... worried... scared even. But I think that It's not about what we feel anymore! It's about our home! Dustin Sparks, Mum, Dad, Chetan and his tribe, Mel, Squint and Captain Smith and the crew, Mr. Mangoleo, the wizard folk, Amy!" he looked at the crystal, "Are we going to let Dietomorse stand where Dustin Sparks stands today?"

The others shook their heads. Isaac smiled proudly.

"Then we are going to go into the Black Forest and show Dietomorse what we are capable of!"

Isaac raised a hand in the air.

"WHO-SIDES-WITH ME?!"

"I do!" Max shouted.

"Me too!" Samantha echoed.

They all turned to Levi, who stood there, scared.

"Hey..." Samantha put a hand on his shoulder and pointed her wand at his tomahawk, and with a quick word, she enchanted it. Levi looked at her, his eyes surprised and fearful.

"We got this." Samantha said to him. Levi said nothing for a moment, but then, he raised his hand at shouted uncertainly,

"Count me in!" the others grinned. Then, on the

count of three, they all reached out and touched the crystal. Just like that, the garden vanished. Replacing the nighttime beauty of the garden with dense, shadowy trees with brown leaves and black branches. Fog rose from the ground everywhere at waist level. Just as Dustin Sparks had said, they were in front of Dietomorse's temple; hidden inside a cave and had double, shabby spruce wood doors. And above the door, was a stone skull that had large words printed on the top it said, L.D,T.O.D.

"Lord Dietomorse's temple of death." Samantha read aloud.

The boys all looked at her funny.

"It says underneath the skull." Samantha explained, sounding obvious. Isaac grabbed the handle of the door and pulled. It took a few moments. Finally, when it opened, it was pitch black in the room. Isaac pointed his word out in front of him. He stepped inside, but then, he screamed and fell through the floor. His siblings were right behind them. They landed hard on the floor. And they all looked up and gasped. It was the seven hallways. It surrounded them in a huge circle.

"We're here..." Max whispered. The four all looked at the seven halls. Dustin Sparks was right. Cobblestone, Grass, Planks, Marble, Glass, Granite, And Alabaster Stone.

"I'll take Cobblestone..." Isaac said under his breath.

"I'll take Alabaster Stone." Levi sighed.

"I'll take Glass..." Samantha said quietly.

"And I'll take marble." Max whispered hesitantly. Isaac looked at his siblings.

"Let's go then..." he said wearily.

And with that, the four wandered down the halls, as curious as ever.

Chapter 22

King of the Tomb

Levi wandered down the never ending Alabaster Stone hallway and held his tomahawk tight in his hand.

"It'll all be over soon..." he whispered to himself, "Hopefully..."

At last the hall opened into a circular room. The walls, floor, ceiling, everything was Alabaster Stone. But that wasn't the point. Four sand colored statues stood clockwise around the room. On three, there was a short man with a dagger and he stood straight and fierce looking. On six, there was a nobleman with his hands folded and he held his chin high. On nine, there was an executioner, with a sand colored cloak and scythe. On twelve, was a seven foot knight. He held a sword as long as two buses and as wide as a large frying pan. The swords tip was almost touching the ceiling as it looked like the knight were about to swing it. The knight was made of pure gold. Silver words appeared from nowhere and it said, *Say something...*

Max looked at it strangely.

"Hello?" he said uncertainly.

The words vanished, and Levi noticed that a few torches went out. And he looked fearfully at all the statues. The knight was beginning to move its arms! It readied its sword.

*Tomahawk...*Levi thought frantically as the knight was about to swing his sword.

Tomahawk... NOW!

Levi gripped his tomahawk tight and ducked the as the knight swung, missing his head by inches. Levi ran for the statue with the dagger on three. He ducked behind it until he heard a loud *boom!* Thousands of rock pieces flew out and the dagger mans head was gone! Levi jumped up and began to run. He ran past the statue by statue. He ducked every five seconds as the knight swung his sword over and over again. Levi jumped as the knight made a low shot.

"Ouch!!!" Levi hit his chin on the stone, he looked up and rolled over quickly as the knight made a huge dent into the floor.

"I can do this!" Levi said to himself as he got to his feet and bolted for the executioner. He hid low and peered over at the knight. He looked at it closely and he realized something. The knight couldn't move his feet.

*I gotta get behind him...*Levi thought. But he knew the knight was clever and moved quick. BOOM! The executioner got sliced in half! The knight saw Levi, who made another run for it. He swished and missed Levi only by inches every time he made a strike for him.

Levi jumped behind the platform that the knight stood on and got behind him. He watched as it destroyed the nobleman. Levi saw the knight pause and look around. But just then, the knight switched hands with the sword. He could swing it around his body!

"Oh no, I'm done for!" Levi mumbled as he ducked again. He stayed low pausing to look at his tomahawk.

"How will I be able to compete this against a sword?" he asked himself.

Then, he remembered how Samantha had enchanted it.

"My tomahawk... and the sword... slice the sword... in half!"

Levi knew what to do. He ducked the sword once more and readied his weapon. And right when the knight changed hands, Levi yelled and slashed the sword in half! There was a loud booming sound as the sword broke into a thousand pieces! As for the knight, he exploded into black flames and disappeared into thin air.

Levi smiled triumphantly. And then, he saw a door. There was a note posted above the handle. Levi curiously ripped off the sheet of paper and read aloud,

Levi VerBeek, second sibling of the Four Wonders,
You are now called 'King Of the Tomb'
All of Forever Land knows this...

But may I warn you...
Your tomahawk is now a deep treasure
and must always be protected.
It shall be called, the 'Silver Chip Tomahawk'.
And I repeat, I warn you, Dietomorse is seeking
your treasure and if he reaches this treasure,
you will be dead when the clock strikes twelve that
very night, and no longer be known to the Four
Wonders!

With that, the paper shriveled up into scraps. Levi looked at his tomahawk and saw a good sized chip in it, exactly where he had hit the knights sword. Then, Levi reached for the door handle and opened it. Dustin Sparks was correct yet again. There was the dome safe room, accompanied by four chairs. Each chair had the letter of their first name. Levi went to sit in his. He did it, not only to fulfill his destiny, but also since he had passed the test – the test of courage.

Chapter 23

Salvia Silverstine

Max wandered throughout the marble hallway, looking at the endless white and embedded black marble. He felt nervous inside. What if he was outsmarted by the enchantment? What if his weapon tooth failed him? Max stopped in the middle of the hall. What if he died? The thought troubled him deeply as he began walking again. Then, he cleared his horrible thought out of his mind. Ridiculous! How could he die to some stupid trap?

His mouth fell open and he wished he could have taken back what he said. Before his eyes, was a giant outdoor graveyard. Hundreds of dead, mossy trees and bushels were scattered about the yard. They casted dark shadows on the dry grass. Max saw twenty four gravestone, just at the beginning! Like the Black Forest, fog steamed up the area. There were hundreds of dead trees, bushels, dozens and dozens of gravestones and spooky shadows and only one Max. He pinched his tooth tightly with his two fingers.

"Alright Max... Calm down... Calm down..." he encouraged himself with a nod and started forward.

~

No sign of his battle anywhere. He was anxious and wanted to get out of the graveyard. But soon enough, he was so bored, he decided to read some of the gravestones. He crouched next to a tall, black gravestone that read,

R.I.P

Colby Ralpson
1788 January 10 - 1822 May 23
Murdered

Max pulled a puzzled look. Murdered? By who? Then he shrugged and read a short, silver grave stone with long rust stains on the front.

R.I.P

Kayla Murkylen

1837 August 11 - 1847 October 9

Died of wildfire

Max began to feel tense. This girl died only when she was ten years old from a wildfire! What kind of temple was this?! Max began to stand up. He felt as though the gravestones were the traps. No. They couldn't be. As Max began to run, he banged into a huge gray gravestone. As lightning flashed, he read,

R.I.P

Lierre Thomson Goolto DevelDark
1849 December 12- 1959 December 12
Died ?

Max felt a lump go down his throat. Died? No one knows? Then, he froze.

"Lierre Thomson Goolto DevelDark." he whispered

to himself.

Max jumped up and looked around. "I gotta get outta here!" he cried.

"That will do you no good." A low voice said.

Max jumped out of his skin. "Who said that?!" he demanded.

"I did." the voice pleasantly answered.

Max thought and thought as his head began to spin. Who is saying that? He wondered.

Then, the worst sensation came over him. He slowly turned around and nearly fainted. Colby Ralphson floated mockingly above his grave as a ghost. Max began to shake his head in disbelief,

"No this- this is not right..." he whispered as Colby grinned his yellow teeth.

"Oh, but it is." said another voice.

Max groaned, because he knew right where to look. Kayla Murkylen was waving cutely at him and giggling. She had a black robe, plus she had blonde hair that sat like a pune on her shoulder. And as for Colby, he had short brown hair and wide, green eyes and his features were defiantly pointed. Kayla smiled her pearly white teeth.

"I've always known someone would come into this graveyard, but I never knew it would be one of the four..." Kayla said in a high voice.

Colby shook his head and laughed.

"Oh, but Kayla, my dear, he may be apart of the four, but he'll be the first!"
said Colby in between gales of laughter.

Kayla must have known what he meant, because she then burst out laughing.

"Oh your right, Colby, he is the first... the first to die!"

Then, both ghosts started laughing like maniacs and made faces. Colby smirked.

"Yes boy... the first to die..."

Max rolled his eyes.

"Yeah, look who's talking." Colby and Kayla both stopped laughing right away and glared down at Max, who simply smiled. Meanwhile, Colby had replaced his humorous look with a cold dark stare. Kayla looked like a rattlesnake about to strike.

"What?" Colby asked calmly but very intimidating. Max still smiled.

"I just said look who's talking because you died before me. Or was I not *clear* enough?" he laughed a bit at his own remark.

Colby's shoulders tensed.

"What do you mean, BOY?!" his words echoed throughout the graveyard. Kayla looked ready to beat Max to death. Max folded his hands.

"Oh come on! I am wisely referring to the fact that you won't be able to kill me. Quite frankly, you see, when you threaten me this way, you should really figure out a better plan, because if you tried to kill me, you'd only go right through me, You're only *ghosts.*"

This seemed like too much for both Colby and

Kayla. Almost right away, they charged for Max's head, but he ducked in the nick of time. Both angry ghosts went flying into a tree. Angry, they aimed for Max's side and as Max jumped out of the way, he gasped. They had knives. Max tumbled into the wet grass and watched as Colby and Kayla went yards away. Max looked at his tooth.

"Don't fail me." he prayed as he quickly let out a drop.

It sparkled like a crystal and hit the ground. What spawned before him, was a clear container.
Max couldn't believe it. Then, he had an idea.
Maybe, something was inside it. He anxiously opened it. Nothing. Max's mouth dropped open as he stood there with the container wide open. He looked up hopelessly.

Colby and Kayla were only seconds away. Max tried feeling around the container but it was no use. He looked up again and saw the two bloodthirsty ghosts, laughing horridly and readying their knives. But when they saw Max's container wide open, they gasped and tried flying in the opposite direction! Only Max saw them getting closer and closer even though they fought and fought to go the other way. Then, Max felt his heart dancing with joy. The container was sucking the ghosts inside! They screamed and screamed but they only kept going further into the container. When they were completely inside, Max slammed the lid shut. He watched the container fill up with vapor.

"They're gone!" Max exclaimed. But then... *"Hey!"*

He heard a voice coming form inside the container. He peered through the plastic and couldn't believe what he saw. Inside, there was a mini Colby and Kayla, except they weren't floating, they were bite size, and they had the squeakiest voices Max had ever heard. Max heard banging from the small, outraged ghosts.

"Get me out of here!" they both cried. Max went from bewildered to bursting out into endless laughter.
Colby shot Max a deadly look that convinced him to stop.

"We're not all, you know." he hissed. Max looked at him and gulped.

"You mean... I have more enchantments along the way." Colby nodded and chuckled devilishly. Kayla grinned at him.

"You're just as stupid as any other fighter we've met!" she whispered mockingly.

Max glared at them and poked the container with his finger. Both ghosts fell over with a *thud*. Max squinted at both of them, and now the ghosts looked scared.

"Listen, both of you! I can fight anything, a dragon, mage, ogre, just as well as you can! Actually I'm not stupid because I'm the one who trapped you two in this container and I plan on leaving you that way! Good day!" and with that, he dropped the container onto the ground.

Both ghosts yelled 'hey!' in their squeaky little voices. Max walked away and muttered to himself, 'And I don't fly through my enemies.'

Just then, he stopped at another gateway that said, 'Entry to Military Graves'. Above the gate door. Max nodded and entered through it.

~

The military graveyard was much different from the ancestral graveyard. The area was treeless and only had gravestones. And most of the gravestones had flags. Max decided to sing a little to himself.

"The hoards of horrors, the plank and borders-"

"Are pirates at the sea..." A voice finished for him.

Max paused a moment and looked around.

"Who was singing that?" he asked himself, "It better not be another ghost!" he huffed and began to sing again.

"Will I find a battle call? I have no shield at all..."

The voice then came right back, "You probably should leave right now... Or you'll suffer a terrible death. You, brainless boy, will bow down."

Max pulled a strange look, then he had an idea. He'd locate the voice.

"Why am I so strong, but feel so weak?" The voice responded,

"You are weak, nowhere strong, plus your thing has

a leak..."

Max looked at himself. My thing? Then, he unpleasantly saw that his tooth was open a crack and at his feet, there was a spawned compass, comb, and tweezers.

"Great..." he mumbled, "A leak." Picking up the items that fell, he threw them out into the fog and tried to sound intimidating.

"I'm apart of the Four Wonders..." he sang mockingly.

"I don't caaaaare!!!" voice echoed back. Max tried to sound like Colby.

"I'm coming..." he sang, "Getting closer."

"Not for long!!!" the voice shrieked.

Max was almost face to face with the gravestone. He smiled.

"I'm-"

"DEAD!!!" someone sprang out from the gravestone and Max nearly fell over.

A horrifying woman, sallow skin, bony and knobby, she had sandy brown hair that was pulled up in a snarly bun. Her eyes were stained and dripping with black mascara. Her giant lips were coated in red lipstick. She also wore lavender leggings with a lavender tank top with a black leather vest and skirt. She wore a silver chain with a red ruby in the center.

She laughed like a hyena.

"Well, well, well, another brute to the yard!" she called in the howling wind. Max stared at her.

"Who are you?" he asked sternly.

"Who am I?" the woman repeated, "Oh you stupid child! You cannot read the stone?" she lectured, pointing at a gravestone.

Max looked at it closely and read aloud,

"Salvia Silverstine, best acquaintance of Dietomorse..." he silently read the bottom of the stone which was written in red, dripping paint it said, 'Still Alive' And after Max read, Salvia was nodding and grinning, her tongue sticking from her clenched teeth.

"Yes, yes, good, sensible Dietomorse. Dark days those were..." she said softly.

Max shivered. "So, you're not a ghost then?" he asked. Salvia rolled her eyes.

"No, of course not! Too stupid to tell?" she sneered. Max looked down.

"Have you ever heard of a question?" Salvia made a face then, observed him. Her eyes slowly fixed on his necklace.

"What's that?" she asked curiously. Max looked at it nervously. He knew that she was pure evil and he didn't want her to take it. So, Max thought for a moment than smiled.

"I'll gladly show you how it works..." Salvia nodded impatiently.

"Go on then!" she ordered. Max slowly opened the tip, and without knowing exactly what he was doing, he splashed Salvia with three large drops in the face! With a single scream, she vanished. Max screwed the tip back up and grinned. She was gone. A door appeared and it had the words 'ENTER' in bold letters, so, Max opened it and found himself in the safe dome.

"LEVI!!!" cried Max.

"MAX!!!" Levi shouted, getting to his feet. Both boys ran to each other and hugged.

"How did your battle go?" They both asked.

"I thought I was a goner!" they both answered.

They sat back down in their seats.

"Mine was intense!" Levi told him.

"Mine was too!" said Max, still relived to see his brother again. Levi told Max all about the clockwise statues, his new name, his tomahawk's new name, then he told Max about if Dietomorse got to his tomahawk, when the clock would strike twelve that night, he'd be dead. Max looked at him, wide eyed. Levi looked down and tried to change the subject.

"What was your battle like?" Max decided to follow along in changing the subject, so he told

Levi all about the graveyard, Kayla and Colby, Salvia Silverstine and how Max got rid of her. Max stopped.

"At least... I think I got rid of her..." He looked up at Levi who looked concerned, "She was also the best acquaintance of Dietomorse." Levi looked down again.

"Yikes." he said quietly. Then, when he saw Max's worried look, he tried cheering him up.

"Well, whatever it's worth... at least your not dead." Then, both boys laughed.

Though Max didn't really find it funny.

Chapter 24

Clunk and Duff

Samantha walked slowly down the glass hall. She flipped page by page in her book.

If any enemy tries to cause harm upon you, and you are less than twenty feet away, say loud and clearly, 'Alluminas!' demon will fall before your feet.

Samantha nodded and flipped the page.

If you are in a dark room, say 'Luamanis Expresallow!' and the tip of your wand will light up.

Samantha tried repeating the spell.

"Lumin-" BANG! OMPH! Samantha fell back after running into a large metal door. Samantha got to her feet, still surprised, gripped her wand and spell book tightly, and she tried opening the metal door. The door was very heavy so it took her awhile before she got to the other side. She gasped. A sparkling mirror maze was a foot. The ceiling, walls, and floor, were completely glass. It sparkled somewhat of a purple color. "How in heavens name am I going to get through this?!" she said, aghast. The sight was mind blowing and it looked impossible, but she had to take a chance. So, she began to walk onto the glass floor and took long deep breaths.

~

Nothing seemed interesting. There was no activity going on in any of the halls. Samantha had taken lefts, rights, and her arm felt like exploding because she had been pointing her wand out in front of her the entire time. Her reflection shown on every mirror. But finally, she decided to look at herself closely.

It had been ages since she had looked into such a pretty mirror as this one. She stared at herself, amazed at how much she had changed. Her wavy blonde hair in a loose ponytail, going just a little past her shoulders, Her pale skin gleamed in the glisten of the mirrors. She smiled and her teeth looked as though they could glow in the dark. She looked much older and mature.

Just then, something didn't feel right. Samantha's

eyes grew wide and her mouth dropped open. Her reflection was moving and waving at her. Samantha looked behind her and gasped. Her reflection behind her was dancing around in circles. Her reflection on her left was playing checkers with her reflection on her right. Samantha was scared. She started running and passed all sorts of reflections of herself that were doing all sorts of different things. It got so irritating, she screamed and ran into one of the mirrors. But instead of a bang, she fell through. She lay there on the ground until she heard a beautiful voice, singing in the distance.

It was so beautiful that Samantha decided to follow the voice which was going down the hall. It sang,

"Shining glass of many stories of your past...
we'll find what you seek one thing after the last...
Hide your secret identity,
Will you find a way out, you'll see...
that's why we think of you as bait...
Now you need to pray you're not too late..."

The voice died away after that and the hall grew completely dark.

"Lumanis Expresallow!" light suddenly flashed from the tip of her wand and Samantha smiled proudly. But just then, she could feel a cold shiver coming up her spine. She could have sworn she heard a voice.

"Where are they, Chosen One, where are they?!" a cold voice demanded.

Samantha laid motionless on the ground. Then, she realized she was having a vision of some sort.
A woman was fleeing from her house, carrying two babies under each arm. She was running full speed to a large maple tree in the center of a field hill. There was the cold voice again.

"Come out, now, Chosen One... We do not hide from enemies we must face." The woman laid her children down beneath the tall grass and whispered, 'I love you' to them. She stepped out from behind the large tree. A man in a black cloak approached her.

"Stay back!" the woman warned him.

"Lindy? Lindy where are you?!" called a voice that sounded remarkably like Amy.

"Tell me..." the icy voice demanded again, "Where are the four?" the woman stepped forward.

"Gone..." she answered.

"LIES!!!" the voice shouted, "Tell me, now!"

The woman stiffened.

"Then you tell me what you were doing with Amy two nights ago!" she shouted.

"I had nothing to do with the woman! Only Lierre did!" The woman said deeply.

"You are him, Lierre!" the man seemed furious.

"How dare you speak my name?" he yelled. He aimed his hand at her.

"Now... where are they, Chosen One?"

The woman sighed, but answered bravely,

"Gone... For good."

"El Jubacabra!!!" The voice yelled and the woman

fell to the ground.

Samantha awoke and found herself again on the ground, the pain in her back was going away. She knew exactly what was on in her head. The cold voice was Dietomorse, and the woman was Lindy, and the woman looking for her was Amy. Samantha stood up and groaned.

"Goodness knows what was on this floor!" she grumpily said, brushing off dirt from her cloak.

Then, she looked at her cloak strangely.

"Dirt?" she examined the cloak. Then, her mouth fell open.

The whole mirror maze was becoming an evergreen forest. The glass floor became grass, and the walls were magically replaced by trees. The ceiling had become a night sky. Several flowers began to magically bloom out of the ground. The tree branches were so thick, Samantha could hardly see. She pointed her wand at the sky. "Luman-" but then, she stopped. A shiny blue object floated about an inch from the ground. The object had whitish eyes and its center was light blue. It was only about the size of a baseball and blue mist circled it. It made staccato noises. It was its breathing.

"Shoo! Go away!!!" Samantha shouted at it. The thing stayed right in its position still breathing as though it were over a thousand years old.

"Go on, GO!!!" she hollered. She tried pulling an intimidating face but it still wouldn't budge.

"Alright, that's it!" she opened her book and whispered hotly.

"Let's find a spell that will get rid of you- and your noisy breathing!" she looked up fiercely at the small creature. Nothing in the book. Samantha groaned angrily and came up with a plan. She would charge at the creature and scare it away. So she took a long breath and began to shout, but as she looked closely at the creature, it looked familiar. Samantha squinted and raised her eyebrows. Then, her eyes grew wide as she clasped a fist into her palm.

"Wisps, of course! I remember Amy reading about them to me when I was little, they were in my book of fairies!" Samantha stared amazingly at them and thought. "What do Wisps do again? They- lead- to fate! Wisps lead to fate!" she then looked nervously at them.

"So that means... They'll lead me to my battle." The words spilled form her mouth. Sh eheaved a little sigh and then said,

"Alright, Wisps, show me the way..."

~

The strange thing about wisps are that when you're an inch away, they disappear and another wisp forms about a half a yard away. So, Samantha followed the coming and going wisps. The forest seemed to be getting darker and darker and the wisps were her only light.

"Ouch!" Samantha cried. She had ran into a branch showered in prickers. She look ahead and whined. It was a huge, prickly forest ahead. Yet the wisps halted and lead her through it, Samantha wheezed a breath and started forward. But now she stopped when she saw at least more than fifteen prickle bushes ahead of her and the wisps leading through it.

"I'm not going through that!" she hollered angrily at the wisps who made no movement.

"Auugh!!!" Samantha groaned, locking her face with her hands as she trudged through the bushels. She peeked through her the cracks of her fingers and grouched,"Of all the places, you had to lead me through here!" she marched through the bushels and wishing she could cover her ears. The wisps breathing was getting very annoying. Samantha sighed with relief as she entered a clearing.

"Good! No more bushels!" she picked off dozens of burs and once she looked up, she gasped. "What the-" All of the wisps had gone except for one, who sat by an old, rundown cobblestone bridge. He sat motionless, his breaths deafening. He was right at the beginning of the bridge. Samantha pulled out her wand and looked down nervously at the bridge. It looked like it would burst into pieces if you even laid a toe on it.

"Hello?" Samantha called nervously. The wisp disappeared. She took slow deep breaths and was just about to step onto the bridge.

"STOP RIGHT THERE!!!" From nowhere, two giants leaped out from under the bridge and landed in front of Samantha in a great *boom*! She thought she was dreaming.

"This is just my imagination, they're just hallucinations..." the giants looked confused.

"We're trolls, not halu- halus- whatever ye jus' said!" one troll bellowed.

Samantha wrinkled her nose. "Trolls?" she questioned them.

Both trolls were big, hairy, dark green and had big bumps on their backs. One troll was very chubby and had hair circling like a mane around his face, and the other had a very pointy nose and a very warty face. Both trolls carried clubs. Their black beetle eyes glittered in the darkness.

"What are your names?" Samantha asked in a shaky voice. She tried to clear away at how ugly they looked. Both trolls looked at one another.

"We is Clunk an' Duff." the chubby troll answered, he pointed to himself, then the warty one.

"Please to meet you...er... Clunk?" she said uncertainly pointing to the chubby troll.

"Yep." Clunk responded. Samantha smiled and looked at the warty troll.

"And you're Duff?" Duff nodded a single nod.

"Now..." Clunk grumbled, "Why is ye tryn'a cross our bridge?"

Samantha looked back and forth. "I- Uh- I'm on a quest."

Duff stepped forward.

"I quest, really? Wha' fer? Ter havoc our bridge?" he asked.
Samantha stamped her foot. "No!" she said hotly "The wisps lead me here and I have no choice but to cross your bridge! Dustin Sparks and all of Forever Land are depending on it!" she explained impatiently.

Clunk and Duff looked at her for a moment, then grunted with laughter.

"So all of Forever Land is depending on you to cross our bridge?"

"NO!!!" Samantha shouted, "There's probably something on the other side! I have to battle something! Wait... Did you know I was coming?"

Both trolls looked deeply offended.

"What?! NO! We was on'y playin' troll chess, when you called, 'hello?' and you've disrupted our game!" Samantha stopped and looked at both trolls. They looked like they wanted to *kill* her!

Of course! Samantha thought. Every time a person enters a trolls territory, they would be beaten to their death! But trolls only have room for one feeling at a time. Samantha had an idea. She looked at Clunk and Duff.

"What is troll chess?" she asked quickly.

Both trolls stopped glaring right away and Clunk answered.

"Well... Duff an' I made it up. The bark pieces mean Clunks and the stones mean Duffs-"

"We play across a log table." Duff interrupted.

"Really?" Samantha tried to sound fascinated.

"Yeah!" Clunk chuckled, "I'm winnin' still am as a matter o fact..."

"Yeh... But not fer long." Duff growled.

"It sounds like a very fun game..." Samantha smiled. Clunk laughed.

"Yeh it is! Especially cause Duff stinks!"

"WHAT!!!" duff roared, gripping his club tight and facing Clunk, loathing at him.

"Well ye do! Yer so bad at the game, it messes up yer brain!"

 Duff's beetle eyes flashed, and he bared his yellow teeth.

"Oh I'm the bad one? Look a' fat Clunk over here, who thinks he's so bright, he married the sun!"

With a huge roar, Clunk leapt on Duff, and they went rolling down the hill together.
Samantha looked alarmed and ran across the bridge as fast as she could. She ran and ran through the fores, not daring to look back. But then...

"Where's tha' KID?!" she heard Clunk howl loudly.

Samantha drew a panicky breath and kept running as the ground started vibrating, *Thump, thump, thump.* She looked back and saw Duff in the distance. She ran for a tree and hid behind it. She quietly flipped through her book and read,

If you want to hypnotize the enemy, yell, 'Amosfog!' and it will be done.

Samantha grasped her wand and began to run again. Then, she heard a shout from Duff. "I see her!"

Samantha ran for her life, until she couldn't run anymore. She turned to see Clunk and Duff raising their clubs. "AMOSFOG!!!" she yelled. Instantly, both trolls dropped their clubs and slowly lowered until they crashed to the ground. Samantha laughed joyfully and began running

"I did it!" she giggled in the singing wind.

Just then, she stopped when she saw a white light. It was too bright to be a wisp; but it did look addicting to touch. She reached out and soon, her finger met with the light. The light burned and felt like her skin was peeling off. She squealed and felt like she was falling.

~

"Sam? Samantha!" she woke in the safe dome room and saw Max and Levi leaning over her.

She slowly sat up and they all hugged.

"What...What happened?" she asked uncertainly.

"I dunno, you tell us!" Max exclaimed. Samantha just then remembered everything. She started by telling them about the enchanted mirror maze, the song, the dream of Lindy and Dietomorse, Clunk and Duff, the two bloodthirsty trolls and the spawned forest.

Levi looked at Samantha sadly. "You...heard Mums voice?" Samantha nodded.

Max looked down, then snorted with laughter.

"Clunk and Duff?" he chuckled.

Then, all of them laughed.

Chapter 25
Dietomorse's Beast

"Gosh, it's dark in here..." Isaac whispered as he wandered through the cobblestone hallway.
He wished hard that his sword was a torch. It was very dark and only a few torches in brackets lit the way.

The sound of water drops clinked down onto the floor into puddles. Isaac hummed softly to himself as he looked at his sword. When he looked up, his mouth dropped open. He entered a dark, gloomy cave. It was large and circular, and had columns around the walls. Upon a clear stone wall frame, was a stone snake. The whole cave looked entirely wrecked, which made Isaac feel sick. Columns were cracked and some were knocked over and the small stone pieces were trashed on the floor. The snake made Isaac feel tense. It's large mouth hung open, bearing long, sharp fangs and a long tongue stretched down a ways.

Isaac was almost certain there were flames in the snakes eyes. In front of the giant stone snake, there was an old pirate steering wheel. He was weathered

and and had three buttons on the front. Isaac walked slowly up to it. One button had an o on it. Another had a 3 on it. And the last one had an x. Smoky words appeared and it said. *Turn the wheel and then your battle come...*
Isaac stared at the wheel.

"All I have to do is turn it." Isaac said to himself. He gripped the wheel and spun it around once clockwise. As he did so, the snakes left eye opened and a black flame shot out. As soon as he stopped turning, the eye closed and the flame disappeared. Isaac couldn't believe it.

"That's it?!" he shouted, kicking a stone across the room, "Why is it always me?!" he questioned, thinking of how he always had to do everything for himself. Nobody to take care of him. His parents dead. Isaac picked up another stone. "Why is it only me?" he chucked the stone at a wall. Right then, a spine shivering hiss sounded from nowhere.

The noise sounded almost like a snake hiss. Isaac quickly turned to the stone snake. It was still there. He looked down and his body went numb. Replacing his shadow, loomed a giant snake like object. Gripping his sword tightly, Isaac turned around and he looked up, dazed at the sight. In front of him was a huge basilisk. It was dark green, glistening and scaly. The beast had the blackest eyes, and slits for nostrils. As it hissed it bared long, white fangs; Dietomorse's beast. The creature hissed loudly and dived forward and Isaac leaped for a column and the basilisk went straight into the ground. It burst and gravel exploded into huge dust clouds.

Isaac missed and fell into a puddle. His clothes quickly soaked before he got to his feet. He bolted forward with the basilisk right at his heels. Isaac headed straight for the wall, then made a sharp turn, making the basilisk go headfirst into it. Isaac ran and hid behind a column.

"How am I gonna kill this thing?" he wondered.

He peeked around the corner and saw the basilisk free itself, shaking its large head and hissing furiously. The basilisk must have seen Isaac because it roared and headed straight for him. Isaac sprinted to the big stone snake to hide behind its tail, but the basilisk surrounded him. The beast circled round and round. Isaac was now face to face with the monstrous creature. The basilisk roared so loud that Isaac fell onto his back. Isaac shivered to his core. He was going to die. The basilisk bent over and prepared itself to strike Isaac. He looked at the words engraved on his sword.

If you believe it, you will see it,
And if you know it, it can be yours.

Isaac looked desperately at the bottom of the tiny paragraph.

Dustin Sparks

Isaac held his sword tight and looked at the basilisk as it dived it's head. Isaac closed his eyes. Nothing happened. He opened his eyes and realized that the basilisk had knocked his glasses off. With a moan, he reached for them, pushed them on, and thought he was dreaming when he saw what happened.

He was still face to face with the terrifying beast, but now he could clearly see it. In between the beast's eyes, was the Black Forest symbol. Isaac looked around for his sword, but when he saw that it was in his hand, he smiled. As he followed the red ooze up the blade, he realized that it went into the basilisk's bottom jaw! He must have been holding it up as the basilisk dived! He slid out from underneath the limp basilisk. He yanked the sword from the basilisks mouth. It was all bloody and slimy, but he didn't care – he knew he was triumphant. Isaac had done it, he had killed Dietomorse's beast.

Just then, the stone snakes mouth had revealed a door. Isaac climbed anxiously over the body and ran over to the door. Once he opened the door, he entered the safe dome.

~

"You killed Dietomorse's beast?!" Samantha exclaimed.

Everyone was gawking at the bloodied sword. Isaac nodded. He ached everywhere. He wished he had some bandages for his stinging knees.

Levi stuck his hands into his pant pockets. "Why does Dietomorse want people to do such dangerous things?"

Samantha shrugged. "Maybe because he wants to be protected-"

"Because..." they heard a cold voice, "He wanted

to be protected from people like you!" the four all turned around.

In front of them was a tall man, sallow skin, spiky black hair, dark black eyes that were full of hatred; he carried a silver staff that was really a metal cobra swirling around an iron rod. There was a stone at the top that was glittering green, almost as creepy as him.

"Dietomorse..." Samantha whispered.

"No." the man corrected her, "Lierre." Max's eyes grew wide.

"I- I-" Lierre interrupted him.

"You knew me? Yes... you found my grave in my graveyard..."

"Your graveyard?!" Samantha shouted at him. Lierre looked at her annoyingly.

"Yes! MY graveyard!" he sneered.

Levi stepped forward. "I thought Dietomorse created everything in this temple!"

Lierre grinned nastily. "I am Dietomorse."

Chapter 26

The Symbol at its Best

Samantha glared at him. "So I wasn't dreaming then..." she whispered through clenched teeth.

Lierre shook his head, while the other three looked confused. "You weren't dreaming..." said Lierre, "You were having a vision. With your eyes open you fool."

Samantha crossed her arms. "Then, why was I laying on the ground?"

Lierre smiled showing his dark snarly teeth. "You fainted after I used my death spell upon your hero mother."

"So you are him then?" Isaac said angrily.

Lierre shot him a dark look. "Since you are the four, I'm going to tell you a little story..."

Samantha clutched her wand tightly behind her

back. Max held onto his necklace, Levi prepared to take his tomahawk out. Isaac gripped the handle of his sword tightly.

"Many years ago... On October 5, 1865, I was sketching a picture, a picture of a storm cloud with a bolt of lightning and a silver sword crossing through it like an x." Lierre's face darkened, "My parents, Thomson and Nadia DevelDark, thought it was the most savage picture they had ever seen when I presented it to them. My mother called it the 'Mark of Death' and I hated that name. Still do today as a matter of fact."

Max thought as Lierre went on. Lierre Thomson Goolto DevelDark... He looked up and watched Lierre pace the floor. "I was now eighty years old and my mother and father both passed away thirty years before." Lierre scowled at the floor, "I was going through some of my things, and I had found my mother's diary. As soon as I opened it, I was on a page that really caught my eye."

He cleared his throat.

I had always wanted a son who wanted to be successful, and not so self involved.
But instead, I end up with an evil swine, I should

have named him Dietomorse.

"It broke my heart..." Lierre said, staring blankly at the four throne chairs, "But I did like the name Dietomorse, so with the help of a few colleagues of mine, Garendelle Moonstellow, Tiki Vanderveetan, and Salvia Silverstine...(Max's eyes grew wide...) We created a group called the Dark Council."

Lierre sneered a bit,

"Another twenty years later, on my one hundredth birthday, we made a spell that can put my 'Mark Of Death', on my neck as a tattoo. Salvia tested it on me. She yelled the words, 'El Jubacabra!' but the spell actually killed me. Lierre looked mockingly sad, "We instead discovered a death spell. And oh, Salvia felt terrible! She spent another two years on creating a spell that would be popular for years. She shouted the words, 'Salrieate!' and my spirit rose from my body. My first words were, 'I am Lord Dietomorse the Dark'. Salvia cheered and cheered. I had made her my first trustworthy friend. Dietomorse tried using the spell on my body, but you can only use it on a person once."

Lierre then looked disgusted, "But before I died, I moved to Wizard Land, and that's where I met your mother and Amy. Amy was fond of me. Once I started hanging out with her, one night, she kissed me. She told me how amazing your mother was and how she would raise Forever Land back to its feet. As soon as I became Dietomorse and doubled my power, I soon found out that Lindy had children. I knew that they would be great. I knew you'd be powerful, but how would you know without parents to tell you that?"

The four squinted and loathed, "So I killed your parents." "I blended in as one of Dustin Sparks' guards and told him that Amy had kissed one of Dietomorse's spies". "Dustin Sparks was so angry!" "He sent Amy to England, and once she took you out of Forever Land with her, I knew I then had a chance..." "And still do!" he pointed his wand at the four,

"El-" "Revoulusa!!!" Samantha cried, and purple sparks shot out of her wand violently shooting Lierre out the window.

The four raced to watch Lierre fall then turn into balk mist, disappearing. It felt as though the cold moment lasted an hour before a large blue flame appeared at the bottom. The four stared, almost hypnotized by it. Almost simultaneously, the four spawned into Dustin Sparks' garden.

Chapter 27

Reunited

"We did it!" the four kept on saying to each other. They ran through Dustin Sparks' garden and into the tower and kept running until they reached the doors to the colorful library. This time they felt braver than ever before. Isaac opened the doors to see Mr. Mangoleo and standing tall, but worried, Dustin Sparks. When Mr. Mangoleo turned around his eyes grew wide as he looked at the four.

"Bless my soul... Dustin Sparks, sir... look!" he exclaimed. Slowly, Dustin Sparks turned to face the four, who were bloody, dirt caked and were shivering from the cold Black Forest. He didn't seem to care at all; he just rushed to them and they grouped hugged. Mr. Mangoleo was sobbing. "You are all so brave! I- I can't- Everyone thought you'd be gone! Dustin Sparks thought you'd make it, but when you met Lierre, we all thought-" he sobbed into his handkerchief.

Samantha looked at Dustin Sparks and whispered, "So, all our battles taught us lessons about where we really came from..."

Dustin Sparks nodded. "Yes. I hope you will always remember this glorious day."

Before the four could speak again, Dustin Sparks raised a hand. "There's some people who wish to see you again." he nodded to Mr. Mangoleo who hastily opened the doors and the guards down the hall opened the next doors.

The four all waited curiously. There came a loud, shrilly voice.

"Dearies! Oh, I hope my hair looks alright... Please Lord, help them to be alright."

They soon saw B's jogging down the hall and once she entered the room, she cried and kissed their cheeks. She laid down a small picnic basket and there came a smell that the four had been longing for the past two days. Food. B's started to weep softly, but when she saw Dustin Sparks' smiling face, she wiped her tears away, she still had red blotches on her cheeks.

"Oh my King! I-"

"It's alright, Lowe." Dustin Sparks kindly reassured her. B's smiled and moved out of the way when the door opened again.

And there was Chetan and Panamoah. "Levi!!!" Chetan gasped. Levi ran to Chetan and the two boys hugged. Panamoah grinned and shook hands with Dustin Sparks. "I thought you died! All of you!" he cried while hugging Levi.

Then he let go and shook hands with the other three as Dustin Sparks when the door opened yet another time. There was Captain Smith and Squint. Max gasped and ran over to them and he and Squint shared a companionable hug.

"Well ye lucky lad, are ye alright?" Captain Smith asked.

"Yes, I'm fine." Max breathlessly answered after he slapped him hard in the back.

"We were worried1" Squint exclaimed, "We were worried something fierce!"

"Yeah, so was I..." said Max obviously.

"I hope yer tooth worked well!" Squint asked hopefully.

"Yeah, thanks!" Max said, grinning.

"Yer most welcome, friend!" Squint patted him on the back.

Dustin Sparks was about to say something, when B's interrupted him.

"Excuse me, your greatness? May I say something?"

"Certainly." Dustin Sparks answered.

 B's then reached down to grab the basket and showed it to the four.

"I never had a chance to give you my gift. I was praying you weren't starving."

"Well, your prayers weren't answered." Levi said quietly and Samantha nudged him hard in the side. B's continued,

"So I made you some sweets for the ride home."

The smiles vanished from all fours faces.

Chapter 28

The Request

"Wait...We have to go back to England?" Isaac asked in a disappointed tone.

The citizens all looked at Dustin Sparks, who sighed.

"Yes... I'm afraid you'll all have to go home."

Max and Levi already had tears in their eyes. "But this is..."

"This is our home!" Samantha finished for them, already crying. Dustin Sparks smiled gently.

"You will return, I promise..." he said.

"When?" Isaac asked breathlessly. Dustin Sparks looked out the window.

"Most likely next year..." he answered.

"Then how will we know when to come?"

Samantha asked. Dustin Sparks looked at them, his eyes sparkling.

"There will always be a sign." he responded. The four all looked at their friends who nodded weakly.

"Now..." Dustin Sparks began, "You had something you looked like you wanted to tell me, Whatever it is, I will grant you it."

The four all smiled at each other and nodded. And they told Dustin Sparks what they wanted.

~

"You want Amy to return to Forever Land." Dustin Sparks wasn't smiling anymore.

Isaac sighed.

"Yes sir... She did nothing wrong!"

"No. She did." Dustin Sparks said seriously.

The four explained everything that Lierre had told them about him disguising as one of his guards and telling him that she kissed a spy. When they finished, Dustin Sparks looked down.

"So...she didn't even know that he was evil..." said Dustin Sparks quietly. Samantha nodded.

"Yes, sir... please?" Dustin Sparks looked at the citizens.

"Alright." he finally answered, "When you arrive to England, tell her, and Mel will take her back. If she says 'no', then she says no."

Dustin Sparks closed his eyes and around five minutes later, Mel appeared.

"H'lo Mr. Sparks sir.' he greeted him.

"Hello, Mel." responded Dustin Sparks.

"And hello to ye four!" he cheered as the four waved.

Dustin Sparks spoke quietly with Mel for awhile and finally Mel said, "Very well... Come along yer greatness's." the four bid everyone goodbye.

B's sobbed as she handed them the basket of food.

Soon enough, the train arrived by the garden gate, and this time... the four were in no hurry to get on.

Chapter 29

The Surprise

They sat in the front booth of the train, telling each other about their battles and eating the food that B's made for them. Several loaves of bread with strawberry jelly and creamy butter, dozens of chocolate chip, sugar and oatmeal raisin cookies. She even made some chicken sandwiches.

"I wonder how B's could fit all of this all of this food in one small basket..." said Samantha as she examined it.

"Who cares!" said Levi with his mouth full. They felt so excited to see Amy again.

"We're here now!" called Mel. The four all looked out the window to see Iron Gates orphanage. With quivery breaths, they bid Mel goodbye and they boarded off the train. They didn't know how long it would take until they would find Amy, but it was really way easier than they thought. They saw Amy walking down the big marble staircase outside by the fountain. And when she saw them, she looked as though she was going to faint. The four raced over to her, already starting to cry and then their professor let out a cry when they met in a warm hug.

"I- missed-you so-much!" choked Amy as tears wormed down her face.

"We did too." Isaac murmured. He was trying not to cry.

Once they pulled apart, the four told her everything; everything they had done in their real home. They told Amy their surprise for her.

There was a long pause. Amy looked at the train. "I- I don't know what to say..." she whispered.

"Say yes!" said Levi.

"We'll see each other again." Samantha promised.

Amy nodded and after packing a small bag and leaving a note to Professor Macmillan, (She would never understand...) Amy was soon waving out the window of the F.L express. The four all waved until the train disappeared. They all felt strange. They didn't know what lie ahead of them. They all stood there, staring at the orphanage.

"So...How soon?" Levi asked.

"What do you mean?" Isaac asked. Levi groaned.

"Forever Land of course! How soon?!"

"I dunno, Forever?!" said Max.

Samantha turned to her brothers."You heard Dustin Sparks! *Someday*!"

The bell rang, and the four all walked up the marble staircase.

But it was true though. They would see Forever Land again.

Made in the USA
Middletown, DE
01 March 2016